MW01170267

THE CLAY COURTS OF NORWICH

THE CLAY COURTS OF NORWICH

Steve Armstrong

ILLUSTRATED

Exposition Press of Florida, Inc.
Pompano Beach, Florida

FIRST EDITION

© 1985 by Steve Armstrong

All rights reserved. No part of this book may be reproduced, in whole or in part, in any form or by any means, electronic or mechanical, including photocopying, recording, or by any information storage and retrieval system, without permission in writing from the publisher. Address inquiries to Exposition Press of Florida, Inc., 1701 Blount Road, Pompano Beach, FL 33069.

ISBN 0-682-40184-6

Printed in the United States of America

To my wife, Marguerite

Contents

Preface

The following pages endeavor to narrate some of the story of the emergence of public clay tennis court facilities in Norwich, Connecticut. The effort was believed to be appropriate because the game of tennis is very much in accord with the tenets and concepts of governmentally sponsored recreation programs, for it is a game that can be played by both the male and female of all ages. There is no need for leagues, organization of teams, or anything comparable. The only prerequisites are the presence of the participants on the court along with a couple of rackets and a can of balls.

Yet tennis has been a sort of poor relation in municipal recreation, in part owing to the fact that the populace, the athletically inclined in particular, have been oriented toward baseball and basketball, the traditional sports, which require acceptable fields and courts just as does the racket game. Also, tennis has had some stigmas to overcome, for it was played for a long time predominantly by the elite and was thought by many during that period to be an athletic event appropriate only for the female of the species.

Happily, almost complete eradication of these attitudes has been achieved as have most of the impediments and obstacles to construction of public tennis courts. But as the ensuing story tries to make clear, it has been a "long row to hoe." It is thought the history of the development of this complex might not only be a matter of interest but also serve as a positive factor in its preservation. Concern for the survival of the facility can be underscored in view of the fact that a clay surface is involved. And, for reasons set forth in this book, clay courts are held to be preferable to hard courts if the maintenance problem is not too severe.

A knowledge of the history of the tennis court setup may well be helpful in connection with future problems, which are bound to be encountered, and the nature of the construction has an important bearing on the proposition of maintenance. Over the years many individuals have been engaged in this endeavor in Norwich and it is hoped these people and their work have been recognized accordingly in the following chapters. Unfortunately, but inevitably, there are some whose names did not come to mind whose contributions are equally appreciated, for all this has taken a great deal of time and effort, just as the emergence of recreation in general as a function of government has evolved throughout these decades.

One advantage in serving over thirty consecutive years on a municipal board is that of being in a position to observe trends and changes in attitudes from close range. This has been particularly pertinent in the field of recreation, which during that period has graduated from relative insignificance to a governmental department of real importance. In Norwich, Connecticut, for example, the current operating budget (fiscal 1983-1984) is now $277,329, twentyfold over the annual budgetary allocations in the early 1950s, when they were about $14,000.

Such growth in recreational activities together with the associated facilities could not have taken place without fundamental reasons, for the expanded programs must be justified, in the last analysis, in terms of satisfying basic human needs. It seems that there are two major points that can be made here: one, in the highly technological age in which we live much employment is routine and offers little opportunity for self-fulfillment; and, two, in no time in history has there been more media coverage, more exposure to possibilities for achievement, more channels of information. Here is where recreational opportunities come into the picture. Now the populace is more interested than ever in participating in the extracurricular in order to lead a signficant life. Government-sponsored recreational activities and programs will continue to grow as time goes on. Additional public tennis facilities will emerge also, but if the current trend prevails virtually none will be clay.

There's one more significant point to be added in respect to the importance of recreation, the athletic phase in particular, which has some important implications. The mere fact that international competition in sports takes place lends credence to the notion that people the world over have something in common—a premise that should be capitalized upon to a greater degree. And tennis, along with soccer, interest in which is happily on the rise in the United States, is one of the most widely played games in the world, where in so many places clay is the predominant surface. Italy and France, both of which run their annual international tournaments on clay courts, are examples.

I now would like again to pay tribute to those who have worked shoulder to shoulder on the clay courts of Norwich, and also to make notation of a very special person, my wife, Marguerite, who not only typed the manuscript for this book, but who has been of invaluable support in connection with the vast amount of preliminary work in connection with the Southern New England Tennis Championships as well as heading up the associated social events. In addition, her critical reading was most helpful in the preparation of the manuscript for the publisher.

THE CLAY COURTS OF NORWICH

1

Friendship Sparks an Interest in Tennis

Extensive provisions by municipalities, towns, and other governmental units offering recreational opportunities for their citizens have been largely post-World War II developments. The city of Norwich, Connecticut (current population approximately 40,000), is typical in this respect. For example, the position of director of Recreation was not established on a full-time basis until the mid-1950s. There were no municipally owned and operated tennis courts until about that time. The emergence of these facilities roughly parallels that of similar projects elsewhere, the appearance of public courts and associated tennis activity in recreation programs finally becoming evident.

This is not to say that tennis courts were previously nonexistent in Norwich. For some time a few institutions had reacted to the increasing trend throughout the country toward providing opportunities for participation in so-called carry-over sports such as tennis—and this despite the fact that a very small percentage of the people knew anything about such games. It was probably a sort of token recognition of the legitimacy of recreational and athletic activities in human society, although certainly an endorsement implying only minor significance to such pursuits. At any rate, it had become fashionable for hospitals, some industrial and other establishments, and some schools to construct at least one tennis court on their premises. In this eastern Connecticut city there were in existence in the 1920s two clay courts at the Norwich Inn (where sanctioned tournaments actually were held around 1930), one clay court at the Norwich Free Academy, one concrete court at the Norwich State Hospital, two concrete courts (which headed east-west) at the then thriving Ponemah Mills, four "dirt" courts that were laid out on the old Roque Grounds behind the Sheltering Arms (a home for the aged), and one clay court at the Backus Hospital. There were also one or two private courts.

It was only at the Norwich Free Academy and the Roque Grounds that any tennis was played extensively, and this by a very small group, no more than fifteen or twenty persons. There was an informal team at the high school (Norwich Free Academy), which engaged in limited interscholastic competition, all home matches played on the adjacent Roque Grounds courts. This complex had been in existence since the turn of the century when the Norwich Roque and Tennis Club was formed, whose members not only maintained the courts but also occasionally negotiated and played intercity matches. Conceived originally for roque exclusively, first half and then all of the grounds gave way to tennis when interest in roque, or croquet, eventually declined. That tennis stayed alive during this period is a tribute to the dedicated few who worked and played on the grounds, which by today's standards, without major capital expenditure, had little or no potential as an acceptable tennis facility.

None of these courts are currently in existence, some having relinquished their respective terra firma to provide space for inevitable expansion and construction. At the Norwich Free Academy, parts of both Norton Memorial Gymnasium and Alumni Hall reside on the site of the old tennis court; offices of the Administration Building at the Norwich State Hospital now occupy the area that was once the domicile of the concrete court; the west wing of the Backus Hospital stands on the ground of the erstwhile tennis court; a putting green has been superimposed over the facilities at the Norwich Inn. The Ponemah Mills courts survived for many years, arrangements having been made to place them under municipal control. The old cement was resurfaced with a bituminous covering, and the courts were turned to head north-south. However, the surface is no longer used for the game of tennis, but rather it serves as a parking area for the adjacent Congregational Church to which the land had been deeded by Ponemah Mills. The courts at the Sheltering Arms simply suffered demise—owing, no doubt, to the advent of World War II when those who comprised the nucleus of players were perforce otherwise engaged.

Facilities other than the Roque Grounds were never used extensively; the respective complexes were not designed or contemplated on a long-term concept of progressive development. Few, as indicated, knew much about the game of tennis and use of the courts at the hospitals was limited to staff personnel. Moreover, widespread activity within the institutions was precluded—even assuming demand. One court for a large hospital? One court for a large high school? In addition, the clay courts received virtually no care or maintenance. The "clay" was really not clay, but rather fine sand, which contractors and others observing same in local gravel banks perennially mistook for clay. (They still do.) Therefore, it was only after penetrating rains that the "clay" courts approached satisfactory playing conditions. Moisture binds this fine granular material, which maintains a semblance of firmness until dried out by sunshine and wind (which doesn't take long) and then the surface simulates that of any sandy beach.

Introduction to the game of tennis in this case occurred in the summer of 1930 on that sandy court not far from home at the Backus Hospital—known as the "doctors' " court. Father was not a doctor but rather a lifelong farmer until 1928, when he became a building contractor in Norwich. By virtue of the move to the city, close friendship ensued with the son of a physician who lived down the street. This young man and high school classmate not only had access to the court but also a real interest in tennis, and was all for a game every night. (Inescapable involvement in construction work during summer and vacation days precluded any tennis playing until after hours, you can bet your life!)

Old Pop, born fifteen years before the first United States Lawn Tennis Association Championships at Newport, Rhode Island, and eleven years prior to the first Wimbledon Championships, which in 1977 celebrated its one-hundredth anniversary, who succumbed prior to televised sports and who did not see a tennis match until 1949, well after becoming an octogenarian, was not exactly ebullient about his son's participation in such an activity. An unwitting adherent of American pragmatism and of Darwinist Herbert Spencer, he believed that finally after all the years of ideological speculation since Socrates, Western man (but primarily eastern American) had arrived at the correct and ultimate philosophy. The unprecedented advance in opportunity and associated rewards for hard work was obvious proof thereof. Clearly, therefore, the sound of the hammer was in accord with that philosophy while that of a ball resounding from a racket was not. (If he were alive in this day of high salaries and prize money for athletes, it is possible that he might have adjusted some of his thinking and perhaps conceivably gone into the business of tennis court construction. Far more likely, however, he would return to the farm, till the soil, and reread the Bible.)

The Backus Hospital court turned out to be a virtual private facility in the summer evenings of 1930. Never was the court occupied on our arrival, nor rarely did anyone arrive to play while we were there. It is very difficult to describe or recapture the early sensation experienced from playing this captivating game. It was a new world, a new activity, elementary improvement a sense of accomplishment unanticipated in life, and an exhilarating break from the daily routine of shoveling gravel into a quarter-cubic-yard, one-cylinder, gasoline-engine-propelled cement mixer—a twentieth-century contrivance then thought to be the ultimate in concrete-mixing technology. But ultimate or not, energy expended therewith stood for more meaningful human endeavor while that of playing tennis, although not quite sacrilegious, represented virtual wasted energy that "wouldn't get you anywhere." It goes without saying that a possible conflict between work and play was resolved instantaneously—there being, in effect, no conflict at all.

Nor was there need for argumentation as to priority on the Sabbath, tennis vis-a-vis the Church, Congregationalism scoring three complete victories every Sunday when the morning service, the Sunday school, which followed, and the evening institution of Christian Endeavor overwhelmingly prevailed. Escape from the latter two functions was more precarious than unexcused absences from school, since pre-Wimbledon Father frequently taught both Sunday school and Christian Endeavor. The doctrine expounded by him, an admixture of the concept of anthropomorphic God and proof thereof via the argument from design, was rather far removed from sports in general. Substantiation of the existence of the Deity followed readily from the design thesis, the presence of cows on the planet earth understandable because of their function of providing *Homo sapiens* with milk, the green grass providing food for the cows and sheep, the latter providing wool for clothing, and so on. Moreover, the thesis advanced was unique in that it incorporated convenient limitations. That sheep existed for the purpose of providing food and clothing was a cogent uncontradictory hypothesis, but for the purpose of providing felt for tennis balls and lamb gut for racket strings was an inappropriate extension. However, it is probably reasonable to suppose that one needs food and clothing first and a tennis racket somewhere down the line. Obviously, the argument from design or extensions thereof are pretty harsh on the quadrupeds, but then God was anthropomorphic and thus the poor sheep expendable.

Had it not been for the move from the farm to the city, the game of tennis perhaps would have been unknown for many years, if not forever. And while the "argument from design" would have been inculcated irrespective of this, it would not have been propounded in an urban Sunday school setting where tennis was a known human pastime, at least by some who comprised the group, and in this particular church by one individual beyond all others. These days one contacts many of them, but thoroughgoing tennis enthusiasts, real devout addicts, were rarities in the early 1930s and yet there emerged a bona-fide devotee in the pater's Sunday school class. Whether this happenstance was manipulated by the Divine Determining Mechanism or set up in a primordial collocation of atoms is not known; it is known only that the fateful coincidence happened in church.

This devout tennis enthusiast, the late Ted Montgomery, grandson of the founder of a highly successful general hardware store, somehow maintained his dedication to the game, despite commitments in the store after school, all day on Saturday, and the inevitable appointments on the Sabbath. It goes without saying that he was destined to emerge amongst the hierarchy of the church, where he rose from the perfunctory yet symbolic task of passing the collection plate up the aisle to membership on the Board of Trustees, following the prescribed footsteps of his progenitors.

That such progeny of the second and third generations, not having had to "scratch for it," whose lives are pretty much predetermined, are inclined to be less obedient to the routines and rituals of their fathers, to give lip service to their doctrines and go through the motions of reverence to their institutions, is not an uncommon development—evident in this case history. Thus a makeshift private tennis court on Norwich's West Side, in Lucas's lots down the street from the family homestead, had a more profound impact on the life of the young hardware magnate than either emergence in the church hierarchy or strict adherence to the time-honored format of the store. Consequently, upon taking over the business in the 1930s, one of his first moves was the introduction of a sporting goods department, the first in the long history of the company. The department was unique in that its entire stock consisted exclusively of tennis rackets, tennis balls, and other tennis equipment. The department was also unique in that the entire operation—transactions, display, discussion, and philosophy—resided within the confines of the office of the young executive. Needless to say, the smart sales representative of any wholesale outfit, upon observing the tennis racket frames displayed on the office walls, readily adopted the obvious technique. Before introduction of the canned sales pitch, interest was first exhibited in the subject matter so unmistakably suggested, a procedure seldom lost upon even the rookie salesman. The more advanced sales expert first inquired about, selected, and then purchased a tennis racket, eventually and successfully introducing his line of hardware. It was like "shooting fish."

The concentration of the chief executive on the tennis business annoyed some of the long-time employees, who regarded this fetishism as an inappropriate anomaly in the hardware establishment. Additional apprehension and ire became evident when a portion of the second floor was allocated to the operation of tennis racket restringing. Since no store clerk knew or couldn't care less about the implausible operation, it was turned over to any one of the town's few tennis players who might be both available and capable, whose constant trekking in and out of the store, virtual invasion of the domain, further exasperated old-time personnel—many of whom, having spent much of their entire adult lives on the premises, had for the hardware company an almost transcendental attachment. The investment involved in the restringing procedure, a simple vise to hold the racket frame, together with dowel and awls, didn't amount to much, but this was not the point. Rather it was the inordinate departure from traditional transactions, this preoccupation with inconsequential trivia that bothered, and it was a certainty that if old Grandfather and founder could know of this anomaly he would "rise from the grave" to put a stop to the nonsensical operation—unless, that is, he could be shown there was real money in it.

Immediately upon closing the hardware sanctum for the day, the path of the tennis buff led ineluctably to the Roque Grounds courts where he joined the small solid-core group of Norwich players. A respite for dinner was unnecessary, for one was taken late every afternoon at an adjacent restaurant—coffee milkshake and fig bars. Generally speaking, there was something left on the dinner table for a late snack at home, where the game of tennis was decried primarily because it precluded a solid, sit-down, regular evening meal.

Eventually another, less direct, path leading one to the same destination became almost equally routine; it began at the site of the construction work, but wound up at the courts only after the regularly scheduled stop at the dinner table at home. The basis of limited acceptance by the small group of players in this case was probably threefold: church affiliation, some background at the "doctors' " court, interest, and enthusiasm. The tennis, although far from sensational, was a substantial cut above that with the physician's son, but occasionally in the summer of 1931 it was possible to get to play with one of the elite, primarily the gentleman hardware executive.

For the next few years, however, it was intermittent tennis for most of the group. There was college, participation in college athletics (tennis at that time did not fall significantly within this category), and unbelievable summer hours committed to construction work during the Great Depression. Moreover, much of this work was supposedly of greater importance, even apart from the financial aspect, than the racket game, since at Brown University one was exposed to some additional doctrines and disciplines that were demanding to the point that the Roque Grounds, tennis racket restringing, and even the Congregational Church were to become secondary for a while. Summer construction work, for example, represented a far more respectable training program for football than did tennis. The coaching staff did not exactly frown upon tennis, but neither were they enthusiastic about a game that was obviously very poor preparation for so-called "contact" sports. Tennis was at best "something," as one coach remarked, conceding, one supposes, it to be slightly more beneficial physically than doing nothing. Work that had anything to do with concrete, on the other hand, whether mixing, transporting it in a wheelbarrow, manual operation of the screed, or whatever, was far more in keeping, both physically and psychologically, with the violent business of knocking opponents "loose from their shoes." Nor was this attitude with respect to tennis held by the coaches alone, for not infrequently in the locker room or on the practice field some tackle or fullback would inquire about the stroke-and-footwork technique of forehand or backhand and proceed to exhibit a sort of waltz-ballet rhythmic maneuver, which was thoroughly enjoyed by the rest of the squad.

Then, too, there were considerations at the university that inclined to discourage one from participation in varsity sports of any kind. There was always the academic aspect at Brown, some departments being substantially less conducive to extracurricular athletic endeavors than others—for example, the Department of Mathematics during the 1930s. Professor Charles R. Adams, faculty adviser and head of the department, was not exactly a sports enthusiast and almost certainly had little knowledge of the football team or the tennis team. Conversely, the coaching staff knew little of the Department of Mathematics. Yet the spokesmen were proponents of the thesis that there were "lessons to be learned" in their respective areas of interest "that could not possibly be learned elsewhere," the football coaches expounding the doctrine explicitly, the mathematics professor impliedly. But whatever the legitimacy of the respective profundities, it was unwise to wear one's varsity letter to an advanced math class lest the poor professor completely lose his points of reference and associated equanimity upon learning that a student apparently did not spend all of his spare time in the math library in Wilson Hall.

2

Clay Courts Pour from Cement Mixer at NFA

It so happened that the first full-time job for specified cash after graduation from Brown was that of physical education instructor and coach back home at the Norwich Free Academy with office and headquarters in the north end of the comparatively new Norton Memorial Gymnasium over the exact site of the erstwhile tennis court, the eradication of which was lamented by almost no one. And even those who regretted its demise agreed with the legitimacy of the trade-off of one tennis court and adjacent area for an acceptable gymnasium. The need for such a facility was obvious to anyone. The indoor physical education program had been conducted in the basement of the main building, now the Tirrell Building, an implausible facility for such purpose, to say the least. There was some gymnastic apparatus, such as parallel bars, but obviously no shower or locker arrangements. Moreover, the game of basketball was an impossibility—although a couple of basket rims were attached to the walls. With a ceiling height of scarcely over ten feet and posts in the middle of the floor it is an understatement to say that any kind of basketball program, either intramural or interscholastic, was precluded.

To digress from tennis for a moment it might be noted that there were three years of basketball interscholastic participation, however, prior to construction of the Norton Memorial in 1930. But this took place at the YMCA on an informal basis, introduced and organized in large part by the players themselves—Dr. Mace Goldblatt in particular. Basketball then was a far cry from today's amazing spectacular. The "Y" floor was, and is, comparatively small; there was no ten-second rule to speed up the offense; the basketball, somewhat larger than the current ball, was returned to midcourt for center jump after every basket; it was the era of set shots, jump shots were generally taboo; and games were frequently won or lost by scores in the 18-14 and 20-18 range.

Also, there were considerations other than interscholastic athletic competition and physical education that justified use of the tennis court area for new construction. Increasing enrollment and the growing necessity of broadening the educational curriculum pointed up the inevitability of a long-range building program. The problems here were compounded in view of the space limitations, a particularly formidable obstacle at the Norwich Free Academy, owing both to the nature of the terrain and proximity of residential areas. The one direction in which expansion could take place, without acquisition of land in the residential direction, was precluded because of a towering, extensive ledge. (Much of Norwich is built on ledge.)

Thus, for the few who did not forget the tennis court, who felt that there should be at least a small place for the game in the overall educational picture, there was total frustration owing to the lack of space on the campus proper for any kind of facility. Scarcely enough area was available for the major sports such as football, elimination of which would be tantamount to the end of civilization. Tennis, moreover, is one of those games that requires considerable space in respect to the number of participants (a maximum of four per court), and as such, understandably and perhaps justifiably, is generally the poor relation in physical education and athletic programs—particularly in secondary schools. It was then feasible only at some appropriately situated and elite preparatory schools where adequate facilities relative to the size of the student body were to be found. It is true that public or municipal tennis complexes, operating from dawn to dusk, many with lights to almost midnight, get more traffic, accommodate more people than one might think, but it is also true that the proposition of building and maintaining a reasonable number of courts for most schools and colleges is difficult if not impossible. However, for the Norwich Free Academy, an action by the Board of Trustees in the early 1930s led to a partial solution to the problem, if only to the extent of substantiating the legitimacy of tennis in physical education, and the existence of the game as a known athletic activity.

The Norwich Free Academy is one of those rare privately endowed schools (there are three such schools in the state of Connecticut) that operates as the public high school, tuition being acquired through general taxation. The resulting situation while unique and perhaps advantageous in some ways is somewhat awkward in others. For example, there are two major governing bodies in the field of education in Norwich. The elective Board of Education controls elementary education through the eighth grade, and the independent self-perpetuating Board of Trustees, the Norwich Free Academy. To say that the two operate harmoniously in the growing areas of mutual concern is, to put it mildly, an overstatement.

Thus it is understandable that Principal Henry A. "Pop" Tirrell, then in his fourth decade as chief administrator, ran the academy very much as a sole-proprietorship. He made all the administrative decisions, controlled salaries arbitrarily, and hired at will—for example, he engaged an English major in physical education in the Norton gymnasium. He liked her and found a place for her even though there were no openings in her field, and, as in most cases at the initial interview, he jotted down the proposed weekly or monthly salary (about thirty-five dollars a week) on the back of an envelope and showed the figure to the applicant for confirmation. That was all there was to it.

But "Pop" Tirrell, however much a sole-proprietor or however far removed his administration from the organizational regimen of today's schools, was primarily an educator nonetheless. An imposing figure, stout both in physique and heart, he was for many years a virtual institution. Confident, forthright, yet never without a sense of humor, his was a personality and character that emanated mellow wisdom—with the poise, mannerisms, diction, and intonation to substantiate it all. Despite all this, though, "Pop" Tirrell did not espouse a specific philosophy, nor did he try to A-B-C subject matter that does not lend itself to axiomatic simplification. He was too smart for this. One does not survive as long as "Pop" in a position such as his if he subscribes dogmatically to any ideology or doctrine. The same did not necessarily apply to the peers on the Board of Trustees, most of whom reflected general satisfaction with things as they were, along with the implied tenets of the times.

"Pop" as an educator would on occasion be somewhat more positive and specific. "Take care of your job and responsibilities of today, tomorrow will take care of itself," he would say. One gathered that "Pop" was implying more than merely recommending commitment by the student to day-to-day homework, that not only would such dedication reflect favorably on the report card but on society as well. And that society itself was designed and founded on principles such that almost any individual who dedicated himself accordingly could achieve his objective, attain to significant status, and make out in the world—implying also, it seems, along with the pre-Wimbledon progenitor both the immortality of the species *Homo sapiens* and the substantiation of the concepts underlying the American success story, whatever they might be. The implications beg many questions, but "Pop" did not elaborate.

Yet here again Mr. Tirrell was no strait-laced, unimaginative product and spokesman of the era, by any means, for he enjoyed sports, was a good athlete in his younger days, was unopposed to tennis, and, like contemporary Dwight Eisenhower, enjoyed the game of bridge. Moreover, both "Pop" and the trustees were required to face up to ever-changing demands and realities in the field of education, such as increasing enrollment and the necessity for the establishment of new departments and the upgrading of existing ones, as in the case of the physical education program and the emergence of the Norton gymnasium.

One of the areas that received attention in the process of broadening the base of secondary education at the Norwich Free Academy during the early thirties was that of home economics. Since there was no available space in any of the buildings on the campus proper, and since new construction for this sole function not only seemed unwise but also would require and utilize campus terrain earmarked for major expansion, the trustees elected to purchase one of Norwich's old and imposing private homes, which was available on Broadway, subsequently known as the "Home-Ec Building." Broadway, one street and a stoplight removed from the main campus, then as now was fairly well lined with such edifices, typical landmarks of any old and erstwhile textile-manufacturing New England town. Immediately to the south of this three-story brick structure was the residence of the late Honorable Allyn L. Brown, former chief justice of the Connecticut Supreme Court, and a member of the Board of Trustees of the Norwich Free Academy for decades, both during and subsequent to the Tirrell regime. The adjacent edifice to the north, another huge former private abode, is now the home of the bishop of the Norwich diocese of the Roman Catholic church; Saint Patrick's Cathedral is down the street a few blocks on Broadway.

With the purchase of the Home-Ec Building, NFA was of course the recipient of all the land within the property lines, and it was observed by someone that the spacious backyard was adequate in size for two tennis courts, and of official dimension. Moreover, there was also reasonable space for parking and an adjacent bulkhead to the rear of the building that could provide entrance to the basement of the Home-Ec for shower and dressing purposes. In addition, since the third floor had been renovated and allocated for the residence of the superintendent of Buildings and Grounds at the academy, the proposed location of the courts seemed all the more ideal from the standpoint of maintenance and surveillance.

Nearly fifty years later it is difficult to unfold the steps involved in the decision-making process here, or to assign to any one of the principals his relative weight, influence, or credit, but it is a certainty that the project could never have begun to start if it was opposed to the slightest degree by Judge Brown. Probably the fact that the judge had played considerable tennis in his youth at the turn of the century and was the originator of the old Norwich Roque and Tennis Club had something to do with it; perhaps the re-establishment of a court at the academy and the associated institutional status symbol was also a factor. Whatever the case, there can be little doubt that clay tennis courts would be the only athletic facility that one could conceivably envision in such an area, bordering on a hundred feet of the judge's backyard. Concrete or macadam courts would be unthinkable.

So, with a nod from the powerful trustee, the board voted affirmatively, and Tirrell was given the green light—procedure, details, and finances to be worked out somehow. There were no further stumbling blocks, no zoning problems of any kind, the go-ahead signal from the peers all that was required. And typical of the times, approval was apparently given with no reliable prediction of the cost of the operation, no idea of the precise procedure, no knowledge of the availability of clay or other materials, no estimate of the man-hours entailed, and little conception of the ultimate playing surface from the standpoint either of maintenance or playability.

A physics teacher at the academy, Carlton Blanchard, who may well have been the driving force behind the entire project, was put in charge. Since these were pre-bulldozer, -payloader and -backhoe days, still the era of the pick and shovel, rake and hoe, crowbar and sledgehammer, scoop shovel and wheelbarrow, and since the task of removing turf and loam, leveling and grading an area 120 feet by 100, would be a formidable one, it was easy to see that the basic prerequisites would be brawn and physical prowess. Thus Norwich Free Academy athletes, primarily football players, were sought and a half-dozen or so stalwarts engaged—and at a time when summer jobs of any kind were almost unattainable. While the exact procedure, the actual succession of the stages, and so on, are not known here, enough information has been gained from some who worked on the project to spell out a reasonably accurate story. Moreover, subsequent experience in respect to similar projects as well as eventual direct engagement with the complex itself are helpful herein.

The boys went to work forthwith, successfully removing the sod and loam, and exposing a satisfactory subsoil base, whereupon they received a respite while the foreman utilized trigonometry, Pythagoras, and line levels to set appropriate stakes and establish the proper rectangular extremities—the job thus being intellectually as well as physically beneficial for the stalwarts. Fortunately, the courts would run parallel to Broadway and at the same time head fairly close to the desired north-south direction. The grade stakes probably showed the terrain to be less level than supposed, as always, and consequently the next task was that of rectifying this situation. Some appropriate fill was trucked in, no doubt, at this point.

One gathers it was here that the project reached a critical stage—having come to one of the bridges that had to be crossed. Not only was it necessary to locate clay somewhere, but also in sufficient quantity and with reasonable accessibility. Here the foreman came through with grade "A plus" in respect to his first decision, for to his everlasting credit he did not fall for the fine sand so plentiful in area gravel banks that many mistake for legitimate clay. Finally, after search and speculation, it was decided to experiment with clay in and around a shallow pond located in an adjacent town where there was a pottery establishment. The stalwarts were dispatched to obtain some of this blue gray material, a cubic yard or so of which was loaded on their conveyance but not without extreme difficulty. There was a further difficulty, moreover, for during transportation to the Home Economics Building the material solidified and hardened to such an extent that the stalwarts were unable to remove the stuff from the truck. It was legitimate clay all right.

Obviously, since there could be no practical possibility from this source, it was necessary to look elsewhere. The search led to the Connecticut River valley and the brickyards in the Middletown area where excellent red clay was plentiful. (Back probably one or two eons ago, the Connecticut River apparently changed its course, leaving large and accessible beds of clay in its former path.) Arrangements were soon made with a Middletown supplier for a substantial quantity of the red clay to be trucked to the Home-Ec site.

One speculates that this material from which brick is made turned out to be more difficult to handle than anticipated. In order to apply a three- or four-inch layer for a tennis court surface it must be chopped up or somehow pulverized, and it is senseless to endeavor application in this manner unless the clay is comparatively dry. Therefore, in the process of handling with rakes and other tools, it must be protected from rains, for when clay is thoroughly wet it's one of the greasiest substances on planet earth. And even though the arduous task of applying and grading is somehow accomplished, the straight clay from the brickyards is too rich, generally speaking, and as such does not make for a good tennis court surface. When dried out it's worse than plain concrete; it is almost equally firm and, because of the inescapable presence of granular material on the surface, far more slippery—like sand on glare ice. When thoroughly wet, on the other hand, it becomes soft, muddy, and greasy and requires too much time to dry after penetrating rains to the point where play is possible. Clay has many of the characteristics of cement except that, unlike concrete, once dried out and set, it will soften when moisture is again introduced, by rain, sprinkler, or otherwise. It is better, therefore, not to apply brickyard clay as is, but rather to reduce its richness or somehow dilute the substance—all of which requires the introduction of appropriate material, or materials, to be integrated with the clay. (This is not to say that bed deposits already so integrated satisfactorily in the geological process do not exist, or that the diluted clay substance therefrom has not been, or is not, utilized. In fact, the reverse is the case.)

However, the task of breaking up the clay, integrating additional material, and obtaining a satisfactory level surface apparently entailed uncertain procedures and difficulties here. What kind of a mess, for example, would result if the area was hit by periods of heavy rain? Such considerations prompted speculation on applying an integrated mixture in very moist form. Since there were similarities between clay and cement, particularly from the standpoint of working and handling, why not treat, mix, and pour accordingly? An appropriate mixture could readily be obtained utilizing a cement mixer, transported to bays by wheelbarrow, and leveled with a screed. In this way a more perfect grade could be achieved, and apprehension with respect to rain and attendant quagmire eliminated.

Whether or not this procedure had ever been used before is here a matter of conjecture, but in any event the decision was made to proceed on this basis. Yellow subsoil, or silt, plentiful and readily available (which is about 20 percent clay), was wisely chosen as a main ingredient along with sand of medium grade to serve as a binder. A cement mixer was set up, surrounded by three big piles—one of red clay, one of yellow subsoil, and one of sand—and enough water to bring to proper consistency, as in mixing and pouring cement.

While the plan as adopted still forecast an astronomical project ahead, the desired result seemed more certain, involving fewer risks and stumbling blocks. The capacity of one batch from the cement mixer represented but one wheelbarrow load, production and delivery to the bays requiring the incessant labor of three rugged workmen—two shovelers and one wheelbarrow operator. Two additional stalwarts pushed a screed back and forth across forms consisting simply of ten- or twelve-foot wood four-by-fours, with other personnel continually engaged in setting the forms properly, establishing the exact level and grade of the courts—a task complicated by the requirement of an overall uniform pitch that would direct surface water toward a dry well to be built subsequently.

The 4-foot bays, 30 all told, if placed end to end, would extend approximately 3000 feet, well over half a mile. But obviously, since the area to be surfaced measured 120 feet by 100 rather than 3000 by 4, it was necessary to remove the inner form after the bay was filled and leveled. This could be done by laying planks on the poured surface after it had set for a while. However, the procedure left a 4-inch-by-4-inch rut that had to be filled and smoothed later. (It is interesting that at many times after rains at a certain stage of drying, definitive 4-inch parallel lines 4 feet apart are clearly discernible even today after virtually a half century, the courts simulating in appearance a giant grate. The clay mixture used to fill the ruts was probably of slightly different component ratio, or the clay utilized came from a different section of the bank.)

It is not known here precisely how long the clay-mixing operation took, but it is known that the arduous process was laborious and slow, that probably there were times when the whole place smacked of nothing but a thoroughgoing mess. There may well have been skepticism on the part of some members of the NFA administration as well as the board as to the soundness of both the project and procedure. However, fortunately for all concerned, and for posterity, continued hard work and persistent dedication paid off. Soon both trustee and administrator could observe the gradual elimination of the mess, the diminishing of the implausible piles of clay and silt, and the emergence of a level plateau 100 feet by 120. Some reservations and apprehensions lingered when good-sized cracks developed in the dried surface (this was to be expected), but the problem was solved by using an improvised angle iron drag, drawn around the surface by the stalwarts who successfully honed the area as smooth and flat as the proverbial billiard table.

There were further tasks such as the installation of net posts and the now obsolete canvas tapes for the tennis court lines, which were secured by wicketlike staples, but these jobs were comparatively routine. The one remaining major undertaking necessary to conclude the project was the construction of an appropriate fence, and here the hierarchy showed its colors when they elected to engage a fence contractor to install one of high-quality chain link, which stands today in reasonably fine condition after almost five decades. Having gone this far, they might as well go the rest of the way first class. And no dillydallying, for the hierarchy was not composed of pikers, and if they were to be identified with landmarks or installations, even tennis courts, such projects would be commensurate in every conceivable way with the caliber of humanity portrayed by the peers.

Moreover, the surrounding area outside the fence was graded and seeded, evergreens were planted, and the whole place groomed such that even the tennis facility, although high school courts in reality, fitted quite naturally and aesthetically in the sophisticated region. It goes without saying that the Home-Ec tennis complex was a topic of conversation for a while, and there were some who proclaimed the courts, institutional or otherwise, to be among the best anywhere to be found. But Henry A. "Pop" Tirrell, happy the project was finally concluded and glad to clear his desk of it all so that he could concentrate on the important considerations in secondary education, was somewhat more conservative in his assessment. He occasionally would philosophize on the project and once commented to a faculty member that while he did not know whether or not the tennis courts were the best in the state of Connecticut, he did know that they were the most expensive.

3

A Tennis Court and Dynamite Shack on the West Side

It turned out that Principal Tirrell could have commented additionally that the Home-Ec courts were generally the slipperiest in the state of Connecticut. True, there were times when they might well have been among the best anywhere in the state, but these times were brief because the only maintenance and attention the courts received was provided by the Deity, who, insofar as the care of clay courts is concerned, is not reliable on a day-to-day basis. Heavy rains, for example, are not spaced sensibly. The heavens open up at the wrong time, notably at the start of a sanctioned tournament. When the rains do come, the volume of downpour is frequently unreasonable and unnecessary. And the Home-Ec courts, which should have received better treatment, residing on Broadway between the abodes of the bishop and the chief justice, were subjected to the vicissitudes of nature just like any other facility.

Since the Deity was the head and only maintenance man, one had to arrange his tennis commitments just right—that is, if he purported to play on the "best courts in the state of Connecticut." This would be shortly after the right kind of rain, like one from midnight to dawn of the slow-penetrating variety. Excellent playability would prevail under such circumstances for most of the ensuing day. A few hours of sun, though, the surface now like concrete again with sand from the mixture on top, and one was inclined to use other analogies to characterize the courts, or different descriptive terminology.

As so often happens when schools, municipalities, or other institutions contract to build facilities, no provisions were made for maintenance. Or there was vague assumption that somehow the problem would be handled, if there was one, by Buildings and Grounds personnel. The only decision made along this line was the establishment of an hourly fee of twenty-five cents for townspeople during summer months. Also it was erroneously thought that this revenue would be channeled for purposes of upkeep. The courts were occasionally sprinkled—never watered adequately, never conditioned with drag brush or roller; and calcium chloride, so indispensable in the care of clay courts, was unheard of, let alone applied. Moreover, no type of top dressing such as the widely used granulated slate or pulverized brick was ever used on the playing surface; rather the covering consisted simply of the medium-grade sand that had worked its way to the top.

It must be recorded here, however, that at this time none of the players, including Ted Montgomery, our hardware executive with the racket frames on the office walls, knew much about court maintenance either. Now, having resumed play primarily at the Home-Ec, all Ted knew was that the courts were generally too dry and slippery, that they played well after rains, that they needed consistent moisture. He sold calcium chloride in his store, but tennis supplier and enthusiast that he was, the commodity was not stocked or sold for court maintenance purposes—nor was it conceived of as a product for such use. It wasn't until some two decades later, when no doubt the chloride was additionally stocked for this sole purpose, that knowledge and use of the chemical had been effected. In fact, the absence of this vital substance (important as a binder and preservative in addition to the simple function of elimination of dust), and the consequent poor condition of the courts, was in part responsible for the start of that succession of events that culminated in the eventual return to Broadway, many years later.

But the condition of the courts was not the only factor that caused exodus from the Home-Ec complex. Rather it was the inexorable law apparently laid down by the Deity and devoutly upheld by the hierarchy that precluded play on the Sabbath, and for the whole twenty-four hours of the holy day. The tennis facility, surrounded by churches, deacons, and trustees, both of church and school, yet designed for sport, was understandably closed during the Sunday morning services and the procession of clergy, peers, and other regular churchgoers moving to and from their respective sanctums on Broadway, but the enforced preclusion of this healthy endeavor in the afternoon was the clincher for Montgomery. Thus the hardware magnate, a trustee of the church himself, sought facilities elsewhere. And there ensued weekly trips, quite as regular and with solemnity almost comparable to the Sunday morning trek on Broadway, to courts at Connecticut College for Women in New London, to those at the Griswold Hotel in Groton, to Groton Long Point—anywhere facilities could be found available on the Sabbath. Clearly tennis, having been for many years subservient to Congregationalism, was beginning to emerge on equal terms and actually to prevail during summer months.

The regular Sunday excursion, however, had its disadvantages, and it became increasingly apparent that for adequate tennis on the holy day this routine would not work out satisfactorily in the long run. Sometimes it was impossible to play very much, and additionally, the facilities were too far afield—all of which prompted prolonged speculation on the part of the executive, speculation and thinking in terms of a private court.

It had occurred to him that the hardware company owned about three acres of land on the West Side adjoining the old homestead, which by now had been sold, a new residence having been acquired on the north side of town not far from the elite of the Home-Ec area. This land off West Side's Forest Street, a dead end and the absolute antithesis of Broadway in every respect, was retained by the hardware company for a unique yet specific purpose. For many years dynamite had been stocked and sold in the store proper, but by this time a regulation had been passed stating that the explosive could be housed only in an approved area in a satisfactory structure removed by a certain minimum distance from other buildings. Since the three-acre tract satisfied all the requirements, arrangements were made with a local contractor to construct an appropriate storage building in the geometric center of the place. It is not known here whether such an edifice had ever in history been built by humankind, or that law or regulation prescribed the specifications. Whatever the case, the uncomplex structure, known as the "Dynamite Shack," turned out to be nothing but a ten-foot cubicle, all six sides of which—floor, ceiling, and the four walls—were comprised of poured concrete one foot thick. One of the walls contained a steel door, locked and unlocked with a gigantic key comparable to that to any major city.

Needless to say, the presence of the Dynamite Shack in the center of this tract presented problems for one who might contemplate a private tennis court on the site. But there were further and more serious difficulties, for after all, the hardware company could at any time cease the dynamite operation. Rather it was the prohibitive nature and appurtenances of the impossible terrain that stood in the way, a sight that would turn away practically any wishful-thinking optimist at first glance—except Montgomery. From east to west there was difference in elevation of some sixty feet, the terrain sloping down a precipitous bank (a convenient unauthorized area dumping ground) toward an unkempt brook and property line on the opposite side, which bordered on a city-owned gravel bank. The brook emerged from, and apparently was fed by, a sizable swamp to the south. And a dilapidated building suggesting imminent collapse somehow stood at the northeast corner of Forest Street, next to which there was a sort of pathlike driveway that selected store personnel would use to get dynamite for customers. Any thinking person contemplating such a project might well start by igniting the dynamite, obliterating the area, and beginning from scratch.

The only piece of land on the site with any potential for the coveted tennis court was a side-hill section between the Dynamite Shack and the huge bank—where some area resident had been given permission to maintain a small cornfield. But to come up with a level place, even an inadequate 100 feet by 50, involved either digging appreciably into the bank or moving the Dynamite Shack. The hardware executive elected to dig into the bank.

While he was well familiar with all the available tools for the undertaking, including their respective price tags, his connection and identification with them had been understandably limited to that of middleman, between the manufacturers and the farmers and contractors, with whom he dealt so successfully, but for whom he had never worked directly. He therefore was not the most productive workman with pick and shovel of his time. But he had other things going for him, namely, patience, perseverance, and unlimited access to brand-new tools from the hardware store.

In the course of living out his life, one occasionally witnesses anomalies or implausible pursuits, and a lot of people have "bitten off more than they can chew" in this world, but this one has got to rank high on the all-time list. Probably it was a good thing the hardware company president did not have much of a background in ditch digging or making plateaus out of hills, for otherwise no doubt he would never have tackled the prodigious bank and lopsided cornfield with pick and shovel. Whatever the case, he proceeded to take a crack at both, transporting wheelbarrow loads of terra firma from high elevations to the low, even though at a pace that would require several decades before the first tennis ball could be stroked. Yet he persisted, spending lunch hours, evenings, and Sundays at the task. Sometimes a sympathetic store clerk would pitch in on holidays, and not infrequently a couple of tennis friends would lend a hand.

By late in the summer of 1937, the operation having been under way since spring, not only was some progress in evidence, but the degree of dedication of the principal was so apparent, it was foolhardy to assume the project would ever be scotched. It was at this point that tennis friends decided to help out in earnest. A manually operated scoop shovel with wooden handles, normally drawn by horses, but here by a hardware company truck, did wonders one Sunday afternoon, wiping out the entire cornfield. A few more workouts with the same equipment and the desired section of the bank was down. Moreover, the gravellike material so obtained turned out to be excellent fill, supposedly, and the men were thus stimulated to level and grade the hodgepodge in subsequent work sessions.

The area was not really large enough, somewhat less than the 120 feet in length needed for adequate backcourt space, and there wouldn't be much open surface outside the court proper on the sides (quite important—particularly for doubles play), but this didn't bother Mr. Montgomery, for later on he could dig further to the south if necessary, and, what was more, he didn't care too much for doubles anyway. Moreover, the Dynamite Shack was perilously close to the court, its proximity presenting a continual hazard. It was not the explosives contained within that made for apprehension, but rather the danger of running into one of the concrete walls. For some, though, the presence of dynamite on the premises created a state of panic, turning away a few tennis buffs who otherwise might have pitched in. The hardware tycoon had no fear of the explosives, which he had handled for much of his life; in fact, empty space in the shack was ideal for keeping tools, shovels, picks, hoes, and crowbars which were stacked at the end of work sessions against the cases of dynamite, which Montgomery tossed around as any other carton of merchandise in the store.

The base of the eventual tennis court at long last established and leveled, it was now time to begin the more interesting task of applying the playing surface. For many reasons clay would be the only possibility, but primarily because it was the only surface material that could be applied and handled in a do-it-yourself manner. Any type of hard court was ruled out, particularly at this point in time when sophisticated machinery and equipment for laying down concrete or macadam courts was almost nonexistent. Moreover, in that prewar period of the 1930s all-weather asphalt-composition courts, like Laykold or Grasstex, Surfix or Duraturf, were unheard of. It would be decades before acrylic surface and finish systems for bituminous were available. And even if any or all of these innovations were in fact on the market, a makeshift, homemade clay court would have been the choice in any event. It was the only material that would fit the limitations and conditions of this private court project. Also, many are the tennis players who prefer clay, assuming unlimited options, over any of the hard tops—particularly during midsummer. Among other factors, it's primarily the continual problem of maintaining clay facilities that has caused schools, municipalities, and other establishments to move in the direction of concrete and asphalt-composition courts.

No one was then at all knowledgeable about clay or very

familiar with the Home-Ec tennis construction on Broadway. But there was unanimity of opinion on one thing, namely, that we would not proceed with any similar concrete-mixing operation. Impatient, anxious to conclude the project and get to the business of hitting tennis balls, tired of pick and shovel, the men were determined to step up the pace and win the victory with dispatch. In addition, everyone was in a perfect state of body and mind, physically and psychologically, to make the colossal blunder. The adjacent city-owned gravel bank was close at hand and pockets of that claylike material were abundant and accessible, not only free of stones and easy to handle, but free of charge. While deep down Montgomery perhaps knew that it wouldn't work out, there might be a chance, but, if not, it was highly probable that something could be added or integrated successfully at a subsequent time.

The job was accomplished with dispatch all right, and in one weekend. With the help of a couple of tennis-playing volunteers, unafraid of dynamite, and commandeering a hardware store delivery truck for transportation, many cubic yards were conveyed the 200 feet or so to the site in late summer of 1937. (The "clay" had to be shoveled off, as well as on, the pick-up, for the hardware company did not own a dump truck.) Although no one could be sure of the efficacy of the operation, characterized and motivated more by impatience than studied approach, there was certainty of one thing, of which our respective physiques constantly reminded us. It may not have been the most effective or productive weekend, but it was the most difficult and backbreaking.

And we could be certain of yet one other thing: that the hardware magnate had come up with a first—namely, a tennis court unique not only on planet earth but in the entire universe, for as everyone knows, although nothing can be laid down absolutely, the possibilities of the existence of earthlike planets throughout the galaxies are probably infinite, and of comparable civilizations as well. It follows that possibilities of tennis courts elsewhere are also great, thousands, perhaps millions, seventy-eight feet by thirty-six, but infinity to the nth power does not admit of the possibility of the existence of another solitary court anywhere, at any time, with a concrete storage shed ten feet from the doubles alley and loaded to the brim with TNT.

4

Tennis Scores a Victory over Dynamite

The facility, however, turned out to be unique in respects other than the proximity of dynamite, for it would also rank close to the top of the list of the worst in the universe. The backcourts were inadequate; the shack was too close; the "clay" surface was ridiculous, never firm except after rain, bounces were unreliable; the layout was improper, heading closer to east-west than north-south, visibility poor because of shadows, and one player looked constantly and directly into the sun except at high noon—all of which caused the hardware czar to return to the drawing board, resume speculation, and wrack mind and imagination as to how to improve the situation. Acceptable clay could be introduced and the playing surface upgraded, but this would be throwing good money and effort after bad in light of the other inadequacies.

About this time, however, the Deity stepped into the picture, and in a manner that profoundly influenced both the thinking of the principal and the future of the entire complex. Whether by design or some sort of retribution, no one knew, atmospheric conditions became such one day that fall as to cause precipitation of the cloudburst type in the eastern Connecticut area. And Forest Street, far from being spared, was hit unmercifully. The torrential rains collapsed much of the additional and undesired section of the bank, in part from adjoining property, causing a small earth slide sufficient to bury about half the playing surface with up to two feet of gravel and miscellaneous debris. Probably most any youngster would have known at the outset that the remaining bank, now more precipitous than before, would not withstand heavy downpours without a retaining wall, but like the "clay" from the city gravel bank, the lesson had to be learned the hard way.

It turned out that the apparent fiasco was a blessing in disguise, for it pointed up conclusively the folly of the effort to come up with a tennis court between the Dynamite Shack and the property line on top of the hill. And since it would be unwise and impractical for a structure to reside on the playing surface proper, it became undeniably clear that in no way could a satisfactory court be laid out on the plot with the shack at its midpoint.

It was at this stage that the hardware executive, difficult though it was, decided on another major break from tradition—the first since the establishment of the "sporting goods department." There would be a cessation of the dynamite operation, no matter the impact on a business renowned for unequaled inventory (more than 50,000 separate items), and the shack moved far enough from the center, a distance precluding its use as a storage for explosives, that an acceptable facility could be built. Clearly tennis had scored the victory over dynamite.

The contemplated resting place, about fifty feet down the slope toward Forest Street, was still predicated upon use of the concrete cubicle for storage, but now exclusively for tools and equipment attendant to tennis court maintenance, detracting significantly but not completely from its absolute uniqueness, for the laws of probability, without doubt, verify that such a utility building, with solid concrete walls, steel door, and no windows, except for small breathing grates, has the possibility of being but a single occurrence.

However, the task of moving the Dynamite Shack would not be a simple one, certainly one that defied treatment with levers or crowbars, or any of the myriad devices, gadgets, tractors, or trucks used, stocked, or sold in the hardware operation. Obviously, the structure with a density, full or empty, approaching that of a "black hole," could be relocated only by a fairly sophisticated engineer who, in return, would require more than good will, hardware merchandise, or the privilege of playing tennis on the imaginary court. Here, once again, Mr. Hardware departed from yet another tradition when he forthwith coughed up substantial cash on the barrel head after negotiating with an appropriate contractor who did the job.

One perhaps might not consider such a move either radical or a significant break with tradition, but to sit down and write out a check for such a project in the name of a sport, and tennis no less, was unquestionably so regarded in the mid-thirties. In fact, this viewpoint, almost ideology, persists to some degree even today in the second half of the twentieth century. It reflects the early morning pounding-of-the-hammer thesis, the hard-work-no-play ethic, the doctrine that sports activities, although tolerable, represent wasted energy in the final analysis—and much more. The emergence of allocation of revenue by local governments for athletic facilities and playgrounds, the introduction of departments of recreation, and associated recognition as legitimate governmental functions were hardly in evidence when the Dynamite Shack was relocated. In those days it was considered by many to be almost sacrilegious to employ major human resources, energy, or equipment for playfields of any kind. It was all right to concentrate on sport to a point, at the appropriate time and place, it was okay to contribute on a part-time or voluntary basis to recreational projects, but to go so far as utilizing the best available skills and machinery to construct a private facility was vaguely regarded as unpatriotic. Thus the hardware executive, the relocation of the Dynamite Shack now a fait accompli, had little choice except to face up to the task of relocating the tennis court itself—on holidays, after hours, noontimes, with the same traditional, acceptable, and timeworn tools, namely, pick, rake, wheelbarrow, shovel, and hoe—a gigantic proposition since little of the area leveled for the original project would fall within the contemplated layout for the new court.

Moreover, the untold wheelbarrow loads and laborious hours involved in the original operation apparently having gone for naught, the proposition of filling in the side-hill section between the erstwhile site of the Dynamite Shack and the brook presented psychological as well as pick-and-shovel problems. It's understandably difficult to engender enthusiasm for such a monstrous undertaking the second time around. But the reality of the situation became gradually to be accepted by the executive, who soon rose to the occasion and once again proceeded to tackle the bank—this time at the south end of the property where adequate fill was available. Unquestionably, hardware resided not only in the store proper, but within the protoplasm of the company president as well.

Once the job had been started, after the transportation of a few wheelbarrow loads of terra firma, those who were close to the situation could not fail to observe not only the seriousness of the renewed effort by Montgomery but also an increased intensity of dedication. Moreover, there would be no respite at the conclusion of the autumn months even after appreciable frost penetrated the ground, for the man of hardware would not be deterred. He developed a system of tunneling under the frozen shelf, sometimes lighted fires to thaw out a deposit, and managed to maintain steady if sometimes minimal accomplishment. And though a noon-hour's work resulted in the removal of but one wheelbarrow load, the magic number was nonetheless reduced to "n" minus one.

By mid-spring of the ensuing year progress was such that the filling and grading of the area for the purported court gradually became less and less imaginary. Now, as in the case of many human pursuits, a few more tennis friends climbed aboard the bandwagon and the site was eventually leveled about midsummer. Hickory fence posts were then installed on the north, south, and west boundaries of the court (the latter very important because of the adjacent brook), and fencing from the hardware store erected in due course.

Everything was then set except for the playing surface, which would not be comprised of the "clay" from the city gravel bank this time. And again the cement mixer operation as in the case of the Home-Ec courts on Broadway was ruled out. Too much energy, effort, and time had been consumed for even the patient and dedicated heart of Mr. Hardware himself to face up to this. There must be an easier way.

Since the yellow subsoil, so plentiful in the eastern Connecticut area, was an appropriate material to integrate with legitimate clay, why not truck in forty or fifty cubic yards of this silt, proceed to level and grade the subsoil across the base as though for final application, then subsequently, somehow, introduce enough real clay to stiffen the surface? The approach not only seemed logical and practical, but also could well both duplicate the result of the mixing procedure and eliminate much of the backbreaking labor involved. Forthwith, Montgomery arranged for delivery of the subloam to the Forest Street Site. He then dispatched company trucks to the Connecticut River valley brickyards for the rich red clay. The speculation was that after drying and breaking up the brick red clay it could be broadcast and rolled into the subsoil with a hand roller. While the idea was not too farfetched, it turned out to be difficult to execute in practice—primarily, because of periodic rains. All of this led to additional speculation and eventually to treatment of the clay in moist form and smoothing with a hand trowel as on a poured concrete floor. After selected sections were treated accordingly and with satisfactory results, the ultimate decision was easy to reach. Simply scarify the subsoil base and hand trowel the clay into the surface. It worked—despite the fact that the operation was substantially more backbreaking and time consuming than anticipated.

Thus, at long last, the hardware executive had come up with a satisfactory facility, heading close to north-south with adequate backcourts, reasonably good playing surface, and even an ample parking area, the area between the previous location of the Dynamite Shack and the bank that once was the original court. The untold wheelbarrow loads and laborious hours, it developed, had not gone for naught after all. Moreover, the now proud owner, and rightly so, of a private tennis court was, perhaps unwittingly, the recipient of some other pleasant surprises. Not only did the final setup make for natural backgrounds at both ends, but since the court was built in a virtual hollow it was protected from disturbing winds, unlike many country club courts perennially constructed at the highest area of elevation. Moreover, because points of reference were clearly provided on all sides, the place tended to simulate a one-court indoor complex, sound waves from impact of ball against racket rebounding from the adjacent hills. In addition, there were no distractions such as tennis balls rolling in from other courts and no moving objects in the background—cars, trucks, passersby, dogs, or spectators. It is true there were some disadvantages, for conditions were so ideal that anyone who played there consistently inclined to be annoyed when playing elsewhere. In short, the Forest Street buffs were a spoiled group who found it difficult to adjust in tournaments at places like Amherst or Williams College with batteries of a dozen or more courts side by side.

But the foremost advantage was precisely what the hardware executive had in mind all along; namely, that a tennis match could be scheduled and played at will, and proceed to arbitrary conclusion. Also, since the facility was out in the boondocks, far removed from the sanctum sanctorum on Broadway, extended play could take place in comparative privacy well out of range of those perennial observers who specialized in disseminating theories to the effect that all the general manager of the historic hardware company did or cared about was playing tennis.

For the most part, there was a void of spectators from the beginning, and even the pick-and-shovelers turned out to be poor observers themselves, at least from advantageous perspective, for it wasn't until the project was nearly complete that time-out was taken for a good look from the top of the hill. During the operation, the only perspective had been from ground level, the major preoccupation being that of somehow leveling that ground. It was a sight to behold, so far different from the once implausible spectacle of the shack, the sidehill cornfield, the banks to the south and east, and it was hard to believe that the transformation of the place, with tennis court now close to the center, had been accomplished almost in entirety with pick, wheelbarrow, and shovel. One didn't need or want publicity or pats on the back. Self-satisfaction was enough.

Yet, while the view of the area from the hill was impressive, particularly for Montgomery, it was so regarded primarily because of the story brought to mind—the untold wheelbarrow loads, the earth slide, and the second time around. To be sure, it was a minute facility when compared, for example, to the complex at the West Side Tennis Club, Forest Hills, Long Island, until recently the site of the United States championships, a view of which from the top row of the stadium would make this one appear almost infinitesimal, but for the hardware executive and a few others the West Side Tennis Court on Forest Street, Norwich, Connecticut, erstwhile abode of

TNT, was more significant, impressive, and something of beauty. And though aesthetic attributes are not built-in properties of the object viewed, beauty residing in the eye of the beholder, almost anyone, tennis enthusiast or not, would be impressed with the sight from this perspective of the court in a hollow valley on the West Side.

5

West Side Court after World War II

Despite the sense of satisfaction and fulfillment experienced by the limited few, the central fact remained that Montgomery did not knock himself out building the court as an exercise in aesthetics. Rather the effort was exerted that a facility for the privilege of playing tennis would emerge. Nor was this aspect of the West Side Tennis Court lost upon the "solid core" from the Roque Grounds and the Home-Ec complex, both of which by now had suffered considerable deterioration. And there were no restrictions, so long as one used the establishment in accordance with the purpose for which it was intended. (It goes without saying, the place was ideally suited for certain other activities—unrelated to tennis. The court proper, for example, was a convenient bicycling arena for area adolescents!)

The renewed interest and participation in the game afforded by the West Side Tennis Court, now a quasi-public facility, turned out to be shortlived, however, for tennis could not very well flourish in the turbulent atmosphere prior to Pearl Harbor and World War II, to say nothing of the immediately ensuing years. Needless to point out, the impact of the worldwide confrontation was such not only to reduce the dedication and effort of Forest Street to insignificance but also to remove most of the prewar participants from the scene.

Although there were no real casualties amongst the group, dislocation of the previous pattern of the existence was sufficiently profound that some seemed to have forgotten the game forever—at least as participants. But those who didn't forget, upset about not being able to play for three or four years, came back home with more desire than ever, desire to make up for lost time. However, at the postwar period of the mid-forties, not only had the old Roque Grounds become overgrown, but the surface of the West Side Tennis Court itself had deteriorated, having lost most of its clay substance, which was inadequate in the beginning. The Home-Ec courts were conditioned in the spring for use in the Norwich Free Academy physical education program, but this was a one-shot deal by a landscaper who knew little or nothing about tennis, and when the summer months came around the courts were in pretty rough shape. Moreover, play was still prohibited on Sundays.

It was February, 1946, some of the old tennis enthusiasts now home and raring to go, when the hardware executive himself, finally getting breathing time after the exigencies of operating an important business throughout the war years, sat down to assess the situation and determine some procedures for the years of relative freedom ahead. High on the list, of course, was the resumption of tennis at the West Side Tennis Court on Forest Street, and the initial project to be tackled, that of rejuvenating the surface. Very early in March, Montgomery decided on a course of action, one twice negated in the past. Sure enough, it was to proceed with the cement mixer operation—the only surefire method that we knew.

While psychologically we were in a far more favorable frame of mind for such an assignment, and even though little preparatory work would be involved, a further decision, another departure from any previous approach, was made, namely, that of hiring appropriate workmen to do the job. The nature of the task, obtaining the clay, mixing, pouring, leveling with screed, was different from the early pick-and-shovel exercise and did not lend itself to noon-hour, intermittent, or Sunday afternoon treatment. Moreover, since the work was far from sedentary, Montgomery, as in the case at the Home-Ec site, sought out the requisite stalwarts. Ruling out the high school football players, unavailable at the time anyway, he first scanned the roster of farmers that comprised much of the hardware company clientele and settled on two formidable individuals with a history of getting jobs done, of having tossed around 100-pound bags of grain for hours on end, of mowing away a half-dozen loads of hay in one stretch. And he successfully talked them into accepting the assignment. No matter they had never seen a tennis court, for he engaged the former country boy and occasional prewar pick-and-shoveler to work with the men from the farm and oversee the job.

It wasn't long before the strong men from the nearby rural town of Franklin, both selectmen and one an older brother of the "supervisor" proved conclusively that a background in football was not an indispensable prerequisite for laying down a tennis court in this manner. Utilizing wider bays, somewhat more capable equipment, and a wealth of seasoned workmanship, the job was completed in short order. There was also a helping hand from the Deity, who, unwittingly or otherwise, arranged for excellent weather conditions that the project could proceed without interruption. It could have been a divine decision to cooperate for a change, or a temporary aberration of the Gulf Stream, but, in any event, the spring of 1946 was one of the mildest and earliest on record—all the frost having left the ground by the end of February.

The surface not only came out like the proverbial million dollars, but solidified quickly, and play on the West Side red clay tennis court actually commenced in late March—one of the few such occasions within memory. Thus almost overnight, the Forest Street establishment regained its former status, destined this time to be far longer lived. Moreover, appurtenances gradually were added, such as a water line piped in from the main street, and a very unique dressing and shower facility.

This remarkable installation, designed by the late Tom Peterson, an Ivy League civil engineer, is noteworthy of mention. A former champion of the Roque Grounds, this imaginative, precocious scientist conceived of a setup wherein he purported to use solar energy to heat water for shower purposes. He first obtained a discarded forty-gallon galvanized hot-water tank (even then obsolete) and secured it horizontally on the roof of the concrete Dynamite Shack. Next, he piped the cold city water from the line leading to the court to the bottom of the tank, then erected an outlet at the top from which three-quarter-inch pipe branched off to two shower heads at the side of the shack. The engineer did not contemplate a shower facility on open and exposed terrain, however, and it was thus incumbent upon him to come up now with some kind of architectural design that would provide at least the bare essentials of privacy. But there was a major difficulty, namely, the lack of an operating budget. Yet he circumvented this significant obstacle by gathering up used lumber around his and other homes and successfully constructed two adjoining wooden cubicles next to the shack, each about six-feet square, one for changing attire, the other for showers. The edifice had wood floors throughout, with adequate spacing between the planks so that water would readily drain through, and side walls comprised of matched boarding from about knee to shoulder height. The supply of warm water was adequate for the first two beneficiaries on sunny days; at other times one either took an invigorating cold one, showered at home, or passed. But while the installation was a far cry from those at sophisticated country clubs, it worked surprisingly well, was used consistently, and served the same purpose as more elaborate ones elsewhere, despite observable differences in contrast with other such facilities, as, for example, the absence of a roof—normally included as a standard accessory.

Understandably, the West Side Tennis Court on Forest Street was used almost incessantly during the summer—by area youngsters during mornings and afternoons, by the tennis elite of Norwich in the evenings. But the general manager and owner of the premises reserved all the noon hours, except Sundays, for himself. There was no need to publicize this, or post on any bulletin board, the mere arrival of the potentate sufficient to precipitate instantaneous departure from the court proper. Nor was there ever any argumentation, for the czar of the court was not only kind and considerate, a sort of Philosopher King, but he also encouraged those who wanted to play tennis. There are probably very few individuals in this solar system who have shelled out more tennis balls and tennis rackets gratuitously to those, kids and adults, blacks and whites, who perhaps otherwise would have little chance to play the game.

Reservations at the place at lunch or other times throughout most of the previous decade were, of course, unnecessary since there was no waiting line for participation in the pick-and-shovel effort. The situation at the West Side court, as elsewhere, changed dramatically when the net went up, signaling playability. But this was both understandable and predictable. Outside the preclusion of noon-hour play there was only one other proviso to which one was required to adjust, and only if he was a Montgomery partner or adversary on the court. It was simply the condition that there'd be no changing of sides on odd games. The boss liked the background facing south the best, and there were few times in the court's history that he relinquished the preferred north end.

He maintained this policy even on Sundays when the activity consisted of doubles exclusively. The West Side Tennis Court became so popular on the Sabbath, the benevolent dictator was forced to set up round robin events, which meant for everyone more time spent as spectator than participant. All in all, though, Montgomery was pleased about the influx of players, even if his own use of the court was limited on weekends. There was only one thing that really galled him. It wasn't that, having knocked himself out with pick and shovel, his use of the facility was nonetheless limited at times. It wasn't that he both maintained the court and paid the bills as well—taxes, water, materials. It wasn't the fact that everybody gravitated to the court on Sundays. But rather that it seldom occurred to any of them to bring along a set of tennis balls when they showed for round robin or other play. You both provide and maintain the facility and the balls as well? True, the "sporting goods department" in the store was well stocked, and all the manager had to do was take them from the shelf, but the balls were not all for personal use—they were for sale also. When on rare occasions a Forest Street regular would break down and purchase some tennis balls, and bypass the hardware company in favor of inferior-quality merchandise at a cut-rate chain store, the normally tranquil executive would occasionally react in a manner hardly in keeping with his managerial composure—particularly since he sold USLTA-approved balls to the players at cost.

It was during this period of heavy traffic, 1946 to 1950, that we necessarily and inevitably learned something about the care and upkeep of a clay court, and Montgomery was a stickler when it came to maintenance of his complex. For example, the throwing away of cigarette butts anywhere inside the fence was forbidden, and anyone who did so was reprimanded in no uncertain terms; dogs, having left evidence as sojourners on the premises, were castigated in absentia—all of which points up clearly that the executive, unlike many tennis players, was dedicated to both maintenance and play, and with equal enjoyment and satisfaction.

While the use and advantages of calcium chloride were then unknown to us, there was an adequate water supply and the surface was hosed by hand when required—sometimes two or three times a day. Moreover, there were the ever-present drag brushes and hand roller, both of which were used consistently—by the principal when he could find time, and by area youngsters whom he had trained. It was also necessary to reline the courts frequently, since the dry lime from the hardware store, laid down by a simple hand-manipulated applicator with perforated cylindrical wheel, would not only scuff and blow away but completely disappear after heavy rains.

6

The First Municipal Tennis Courts

Understandably, the excellent condition and the impeccability of the West Side Tennis Court, together with the steadily increasing traffic, attracted considerable attention and from some of those engaged in the field of sport and recreation, notably Simon Googel, superintendent of Playgrounds in 1950. (The city of Norwich was roughly abreast of comparable municipalities in the field of recreation, and although far from full-fledged departmental status, an appointive Recreation Commission, whose primary function was that of operating summer playgrounds, had been in existence for many years.) Googel was both a knowledgeable and imaginative administrator well aware of the advantages of tennis as a sound activity, providing opportunity for adults as well as youth, male and female of all ages. In view of the potential for such across-the-board participation, tennis, though perhaps a poor relation, nonetheless offered recreational opportunities for a broad spectrum of the populace and therefore was very much in accord with what would be the concepts and objectives in this field in the years to come.

Early in the eight-week summer session of that year Si Googel decided to introduce the game as part of the program and sought the use of the Forest Street court for such purpose. Montgomery not only acquiesced but also offered to assist in the program voluntarily and contributed tennis balls and some rackets as well. Soon Miss Anne Twomey, supervisor of physical education for girls at the Norwich Free Academy, and one or two others became involved in the weekly activity.

Shortly after the inception of the program it was obvious to everyone that the clinics would be almost meaningless in the long run without facilities other than the West Side court on Forest Street. The Norwich Free Academy courts behind the Home Economics Building were not maintained satisfactorily during this period. Even if conditioned consistently and available for the general public free of charge, tennis facilities would still be inadequate, assuming a moderate increase in interest—it's one thing to learn a little about the game, but this hardly makes sense if there are virtually no places to play—whereupon, Googel, the notion of municipally owned tennis courts in mind all along, introduced the idea to Mr. James V. Pedace, chairman of the Recreation Commission, who forthwith took a good look at the program and complex on the West Side.

A few words about Mr. Jim Pedace. In all its history, the city of Norwich, which in 1984 celebrates the 325th year of its founding, has had few if any more dedicated and devoted citizens. His profound self-sacrificing attachment to the home town has been, and is, constantly in evidence. A lifelong newspaperman, for many years a city editor of the *Norwich Bulletin*, who in retirement wrote an extensive weekly column about local events, issues, and personalities, Jim's interests, enthusiasm, and energy have been almost unbelievable. Small wonder this man who has served in so many important capacities was chosen "man of the year" in the early 1950s. Until very recently he served on the committee appointed by the city council for the enhancement of Mohegan Park, through which he walks several miles daily. A permanent plaque set in a stone near the flagpole at the park reads as follows: *James V. Pedace. In appreciation of his faithful service as a member of the Mohegan Park Improvement and Development Committee through the years 1973-1978.*

It was easy for Googel to arouse immediate interest in tennis courts when he contacted the chairman of the Recreation Commission, for Jim Pedace, imbued with the idea of service and progress, was all ears when it came to such proposals. Moreover, he was familiar with the background of sport and recreation in Norwich and of Mohegan Park, the preservation and maintenance of which was a matter of the utmost importance for the commissioner. The western section of the park, up the hill behind the Norwich Free

Academy, had been the site of an extensive, though unfinished, Works Progress Administration project during the Great Depression in the late 1930s. This project took place on land deeded to the city of Norwich by the academy under conditions guaranteeing availability and use of the area during the academic year. The plans originally called for a clubhouse with shower and toilet facilities, a satisfactory baseball field, a smaller subsidiary field, six tennis courts across Mohegan Road from the building, and an acceptable running track, which would circumvent the courts. The project was never concluded because of the advent of World War II. The clubhouse building and major baseball field were about completed, but the tennis court and running track project never materialized and was understandably scotched.

Jim Pedace not only knew of the original WPA plans but was also aware of the exact site earmarked for the tennis courts. One day, soon after the Googel interview, the chairman and this Forest Street buff looked over that area, assessing its potential and adaptability. The place was an absolute natural, since at that point Mohegan Road runs almost directly from east to west, thus making it possible to construct courts in the north-south direction and, at the same time, perpendicular to the road. In addition, the linden trees planted under the WPA project along the street would provide an excellent background at the south end, nature having arranged for adequate foliage to the north and west.

Nothing transpired further until about twenty-four hours had elapsed, when a telephone call was received from Jim Pedace requesting attendance at a meeting in the mayor's office in City Hall. It was a telephone call, it has turned out, that determined a substantial part of the course of one life, that certainly has added another dimension to many others—and that conceivably may well have lengthened those of still a few more.

In this important and educational meeting, chaired by Mr. Pedace, with both the mayor, Richard Marks, and the first selectman, Thomas Dorsey, in attendance, it was apparent at the inception that the chairman of the Recreation Commission had given more thought to the project than one would have guessed. In addition to the appropriate government officials, there were significant others present, for example, a private contractor and an engineer, each of whom would be scheduled for a segment of the work, assuming the go-ahead signal was given by the mayor.

When this "consultant" was asked by Jim to spell out for the group the exact procedure involved in the construction of two tennis courts at the Mohegan Park site, and after having been represented as one with some experience in this area, the first thought was to try to act as though one did, in fact, know something about it. Another overriding concern was simply apprehension that the project would not get off the ground. Therefore, the tendency was to minimize the undertaking, implying the process to be straightforward and comparatively easy. All that had to be done was to strip the topsoil together with associated brush and vegetation, level the terrain, bring in the appropriate gravel for the base, obtain the clay, apply and roll same, build the fences, install a water line, erect the net posts, put down the lines, put up the nets—and open the complex . . . whereupon it was suggested that this pseudo-consultant go a little slower.

The beginning of indoctrination in the operation of municipal government, and recreational projects in particular, took place at this time. In the course of the next half-hour or so of conversational give and take, some salient realities came gradually to be absorbed. First and foremost was that recreation as a governmental function in Norwich was still in its infancy, that restraint by elective officials in respect to appropriation for such purposes was still the watchword, and there was no specific allocation of funds (and probably would not be in the immediate future) for this tennis court project. And even if the proposition was so introduced, by ordinance or resolution with attendant hearings and publicity, it would, no doubt, be destined to failure, for neither logic nor political expediency could justify expenditure of several thousand dollars for two tennis courts when the total overall recreation budget was in the twelve- to fourteen-thousand-dollar range—less than one-tenth of what it would be twenty-five years later. Moreover, assuming the project successfully survived the governmental process with adequate funds appropriated and specifications agreed upon before going out for bid, at least a year or two, and probably more, would transpire before fruition.

None of this was lost upon Chairman Pedace, who probably had more knowledgeability than most as to how such an eventuality could come to pass within the immediate foreseeable future. In part, success would depend on the drive and leadership of the principals, but even a larger part on the degree and extent of whatever cooperation and assistance that could be mustered. Fortunately, the timing for such an endeavor was good. Whether explainable in terms of a reaction and concomitant new psychology of the people in the postwar period, or in the gradual acceptance and realization of the importance of recreational activity in a complex society, or both, there emerged a more or less general attitude wherein growing numbers of individuals and organizations wanted to make some kind of contribution to life overall—to do some good. Not that all this was unique or especially applicable in the aftermath of World War II exclusively, for philosophers and humanitarians have always flourished, but more interest along this line was discernible than before—at least in the field of recreation and sports. However cogent or valid these limited observations, it was not difficult for a man like Jim Pedace to round up volunteers for the tennis court job—a job purported to be accomplished even without municipal funding or speculation as to the availability of matching federal or state grants. And much of the groundwork was established that night in the mayor's office in City Hall. The chairman was not one to conceive of something like this, kick it around forever and a day, contemplating conclusion for posterity in the twenty-first century. He was more interested in the present insofar as this and other such items were concerned, and he was determined to come up with something in the first summer of the second half of the twentieth century—though it was a July night in the middle of which summer that the project was really first introduced.

Nothing transpired until the following morning when "all hell broke loose." The Zachae brothers, building contractors who just happened to attend the meeting, had arrived at the site. These two imposing gentlemen, twin brothers who later on were to become "men of the year" themselves, having worked diligently and gratuitously in connection with many community endeavors, had a lifelong history of public service. Moreover, they also had a bulldozer. This monster, though an early model, altered the appearance and character of the area in a comparatively short time—in contrast to the pick-and-shovel operations at Forest Street and the Home-Ec courts. One watches such a piece of equipment in action and is struck by the drone and monotony, its apparent futility, but when he returns after a while he is astounded with the transformation. Thus the first phase, that of stripping topsoil, removing boulders and brush, was concluded in a day.

The site now cleared and exposed, it was time for arrival of the engineer, Shepard Palmer, who by chance was also in attendance at the meeting in City Hall. Interestingly enough, he was also a member of the original "solid core," a product of the Roque Grounds who later captained his college tennis team. He, too, had a background in public service—comparable to that of the Zachae brothers and Pedace himself. Using somewhat more sophisticated equipment than the line levels from the hardware store employed at Forest Street, the engineer quickly established the appropriate grades and extremities, driving in the wooden stakes accordingly.

However, the difference in elevation from east to west turned out, like the Home-Ec situation, to be greater than had been thought originally. In fact, substantial amounts of water would collect and stagnate at the west end of the site, resulting in the emergence of a small pond after heavy rains. It was obvious to First Selectman Dorsey, the next person of importance to arrive, and to Palmer, that this low area where one of the courts was to reside would necessarily have to be brought to sufficient grade in order to give reasonable assurance that the facility would, in fact, be used for tennis primarily—as opposed, for example, to occasional fishing or other aquatic activity. Any attempt to fill this frequently inundated space with surrounding material would be foolhardy because such procedure, no doubt, would result in the creation of a small lake instead. Thus the first selectman, whose commitment was that of trucking in the gravel for the base of the courts, was required to face up to a larger proposition than envisioned. Moreover, the task would be difficult and complicated for him, simply because this was the busiest time of year for his personnel, trucks, and equipment. But Tom Dorsey somehow managed to come through, completing the assignment within a few days.

The number of cubic yards of gravel required soared to approximately 2,000, representing an admirable cooperative effort, as well as completion of an unanticipated task, by the government official. But, since his department was the only one in town or city that had the necessary equipment to grade and roll the gravel that was trucked in, there was more in the offing for Selectman Dorsey. Yet, once again, Tom came through in great fashion, sending the town's comparatively new grader, along with its capable operator, to the scene. Highly regarded by the first selectman, the man at the controls proceeded not only to substantiate Mr. Dorsey's appraisal of him, but also to impress everyone involved in the project. He had a keen interest in the undertaking, working overtime on his own so that he could return as quickly as possible to major commitments on the roads and highways.

The tennis court base was graded and rolled to perfection, and, as engineer Palmer remarked, "You could almost play on it the way it is." But it really is impossible to play much of a game of tennis on just plain bank gravel. (Although in these days attempts to do so by some of the buffs would not be surprising.) If such was the case there would be far more courts, both public and private, particularly in the eastern Connecticut area, where enough of this material exists to provide the optimum number anywhere in the world. If there is a place and function for gravel in connection with a tennis court, it is other than on, or for, the playing surface proper, where material is needed that will pack and solidify to the appropriate extent and remain firm. Clay, insofar as anyone knew, was such a material.

The paramount question now was the simple one of where to obtain the clay, formulation and planning not having reached this stage at the meeting in the mayor's office. The bridge could be crossed by obtaining red clay from the brickyards forty miles away in the Connecticut River valley. But this, unlike the bank gravel, would cost money, a commodity in very short supply. (Or, as some suggested, we could use that fine granular material, the "clay" from the city gravel banks, but having gone this route, we succeeded in setting the idea aside.) Also, application of the red clay over the base represented such a magnitude of effort and manpower as to preclude the undertaking. Certainly the cement mixer operation would be ill-advised, and, moreover, volunteers, civic-minded private contractors and highway personnel, could not be available indefinitely. Mobilization of such a group, maintaining its enthusiasm, is one thing; holding it all together for more than a reasonable length of time is quite another.

Since the existence of this volunteer corps was destined to be shortlived, it became incumbent upon leadership to determine the format for the next procedure forthwith—to keep the show on the road. A breakthrough occurred when Chairman Pedace learned of a clay deposit right in the city of Hartford on Asylum Avenue, a couple of stones' throw from the state Capitol Building. This possible source had been suggested by a brickyard operator whom Jim had contacted, and who knew something of the problem. While digging out for the foundation and basement for the new home office of the Phoenix Mutual Life Insurance Company, the contractors had uncovered an extensive clay bed that had to be removed. They were then in the process of simply getting rid of the stuff, on which it was impossible to erect a sound structure of this magnitude, trucking it to an inaccessible, yet approved, site. Pedace approached the management of the contracting firm who was willing to let the city of Norwich have the clay free of charge, providing its own trucks were utilized for transportation and that they arrive to be loaded during weekday working hours. If the Norwich trucks were available just on Saturdays, which was the only possibility, it would be necessary to pay the steam shovel operator.

Before endeavoring to set up any trucking arrangement, however, it was decided that we get some assurance that the clay under consideration would be satisfactory for our purposes, whereupon it was suggested that the consultant go to the Asylum Avenue site to make such a determination. Few if any comparable analyses have been as exhaustive as this one, the most scientific part being that of driving a junk automobile (which any reasonably experienced motorist would not drive to the nearest church on Sunday) to the city of Hartford. The junk finally having made it to the capital city and parked, not unintentionally, around the corner out of sight, this consultant retained by the Norwich Recreation Commission emerged therefrom, proceeded to the area, and sought out the man in charge. It was imperative, supposedly, to act as though one knew what he was doing, for, after all, you're representing the city of Norwich. Presently, with perfunctory cooperation from the foreman, there took place a cursory examination by the consultant whose only concern as of that point was whether or not it was the same fine granular sand so plentiful in Norwich. The gray material sure looked to be identical, and if such was the case, it would call for submission of a studied report suggesting the inadvisability of trucking in the "clay" some forty miles when an unlimited supply was available a few hundred yards from Mohegan Park at home. However, since some decision was assumed to be forthcoming, the pseudo-scientist proceeded to do what any bona-fide scientist would no doubt do, namely, pick up a sample to take back home to Norwich for analysis. The unimpressed foreman couldn't care less; all it meant to him, apparently, was that the remaining volume to be removed was reduced by an infinitesimal cubic foot.

Examination of the material, conducted along with engineer Palmer, consisted simply of exposing it to the sun until thoroughly dried out, then applying pressure while observing the reaction. If the sample broke down, disintegrating into fine sand, it flunked the test. If it solidified and withstood reasonable pressure, as from stomping, it passed. And pass this critical examination it sure did. Repeated experiments, after moistening the material thoroughly, produced similar results.

Thus Chairman Pedace, the green light having been given by the researchers, proceeded to make arrangements for transportation of the clay to Mohegan Park. There have been remarkable, implausible, and perhaps similar maneuvers consummated in the history of municipalities, but probably not one quite so unique. Ten city and town dump trucks, with maximum capacity of approximately five cubic yards each, were somehow mobilized at 6:00 A.M. on the very next Saturday at the Mohegan Park starting line for two round trips to Asylum Avenue. While some of the vehicles, constantly engaged in daily workouts, were in fairly good shape, others were older and questionable on this score, were used infrequently, and few had ever attempted such an extensive out-of-town journey. Nonetheless, the drivers were not only good sports who accepted the assignment in fine spirit, but, unknown to us, introduced incentive and enthusiasm on their own—in the form of bets as to who would complete the round trips first.

Jim Pedace and his adviser were positively nonplused when the first truck arrived as early as 8:30 A.M. Shortly thereafter came the second, third, and so on. Immediately upon completion of the first round trip, each driver took off on his second and final journey. By noon, half the trucks had delivered the requisite two loads. Not so, however, with the other half, which limped in at intervals well into the afternoon—the tenth and last, having broken down a couple of times, about 6:00 P.M.

Thus twenty loads of this legitimate clay, about 80 to 85 cubic yards (some trucks incapable of handling more than 4 yards) were delivered that Saturday late in July 1950. The loads were spotted checkerboard style over the 12,000 square feet of gravel base, which was chewed up considerably in the dumping operation. Yet the presence of the clay was a fait accompli, and the prospect of a municipal tennis facility for even the late summer of that year, became a possibility. A major hurdle had been scaled, clay having been obtained virtually free of charge. The only expenditure was that of a day's pay for the truck drivers, which Pedace was able to absorb in his recreation budget. No bill was ever received from the Phoenix Mutual contractors in regard to overtime pay for the steam shovel operator.

Before any tennis playing could take place, however, there were two additional major projects that somehow had to be completed, as well as several minor tasks. One, of course, was that of applying an even layer of the clay over the gravel base; the other was the building of an appropriate fence. It is possible to play the game without a fence of any kind, but the absence of this appurtenance would detract considerably from the sport, to say the least. While the two jobs were tackled concurrently, it is best to treat them one at a time.

As to the application of the playing surface, it was first necessary to speculate at some length as to how to go about it. To be sure, the twenty piles of clay could be attacked with picks, shovels, rakes, and hoes. Nor would such a procedure have been too farfetched, for the gray material from Hartford, considerably less rich than the red clay from the brickyards, was easier to handle. But the manpower involved would be well outside the scope of the volunteer corps, and even, given the workers, the days, probably weeks, entailed in such procedure fitted neither the timetable nor the personality of Jim Pedace.

These and other considerations caused us once again to turn to Selectman Dorsey, who along with his operator studied the situation for a while, deliberating as to whether or not the job could be done with the town grader. But clay, unless previously processed, or except at very infrequent optimum times when dried out to a critical point, does not lend itself readily to treatment by heavy equipment. It is either too much like grease when moist or too firm and compact when dry. At this point, a suggestion was made by the wishful-thinking consultant. Perhaps if medium-grade sand was integrated somehow, it might neutralize some of the prohibitive properties of the clay to the point where the grader could be used effectively. Accordingly, the selectman sent in about twenty cubic yards of sand, instructing the truck drivers to dump about one yard on each of the twenty piles of clay. Successive attacks, or swipes, at each pile by the grader made for sufficient integration of the sand, with the result that the clay could be handled by heavy equipment. The highly capable operator completed the difficult task in one day.

Unfortunately, however, some undesirable and unanticipated developments occurred, and through no fault in workmanship. Essentially, the difficulties stemmed primarily, but not completely, from the regrettable fact that the 80-odd yards of clay turned out to be inadequate, in part because it was spread and applied in this manner. As a result, one end of the area was the recipient of a skimpy application—scarcely enough to cover the gravel. While a little simple arithmetic indicates quickly that 80 cubic yards is sufficient to provide a clay surface in excess of 2 inches over a 12,000-square-foot base, there are some variables and other factors that easily fault the mathematical estimates in actual practice. True, the clay might have been sufficient if applied meticulously by hand, utilizing forms, shovels, and rakes, but such an endeavor could extend almost interminably.

In the calculation it was assumed that the gravel base was an almost perfect plane, which, of course, as in most cases, was not a correct premise. Thus, if two inches of surfacing is applied to the areas of high elevation, it is easy to see that substantially more material is needed elsewhere. Moreover, in this situation, given that the assumption was valid, that the base was almost perfect at the outset, it wasn't long after a few passes at the rugged piles of clay by the town grader that the base, which looked so good, lost all resemblance to a plane of any kind.

The grader operator had started at the north end of the site, working, spreading, and leveling the clay toward the south section and Mohegan Road, the same direction of an established pitch designed to funnel surface water to a catch basin that had been built near the street under the WPA project. It was at the south end that the operator began running out of the clay and where he was forced to thin out the surface. Unfortunately, this had the effect, among other things, of increasing the pitch, too pronounced in the first place, to an undesirable degree.

Another interesting, yet inescapable, development took place as the grader operator proceeded. It turned out to be impossible not to integrate the bank gravel with the clay. The equipment was so gigantic and heavy, the base thus chewed up under so much pressure, that this result could not have been avoided. Earlier it was stated that there was no place for bank gravel in or on the playing surface proper of a tennis court, but by the end of that day's grading operation it was obvious that the first municipal tennis courts in the city of Norwich were destined to be an exception.

Integration of appreciable gravel and its multitude of stones with the clay now another fait accompli, there was no choice but to work, grade, and roll this unique mixture for the playing surface, a job that would require somewhat more delicate equipment than Selectman Dorsey's grader. But it was only a matter of time—time enough for Chairman Pedace to make another telephone call—before a volunteer was recruited. Accordingly, landscaper Herb Williams, an independent private contractor, arrived the very next day and proceeded to do the work—gratuitously. The late Mr. Williams, operating his light equipment personally, did a fine job of honing, grading, brushing, and rolling the surface, which came out better than any of us had anticipated, all the stones having been rolled out of sight. It was, of course, impossible for the landscaper to rectify the slope from north to south, nor was he able to add significantly to the thin layer of clay at the lower end. Also, since too much sand had been mixed in with the clay, both from that cubic yard dumped on each pile and from the integrated gravel, the surface that emerged was far too much like concrete, and with excessive granular material on top.

As indicated earlier, another operation, that of building the fence, had been going on at the same time as the clay application. It goes without saying that extensive planning for said fence did not transpire at the meeting in the mayor's office in City Hall, for, after all, the building of some kind of enclosure would be comparatively simple, an easy bridge to cross when you came to it. Nonetheless, construction would obviously entail acquisition of necessary materials as well as appropriate manpower to do the job.

Understandably, it was important first to determine just how much fencing would be required, or what would be the absolute minimum. In light of the void of tangible resources, basic ones such as cash and labor, it was decided to scotch any notion of enclosing the entire area. We settled for backstops at the north and south ends, each 100 feet in length. It was then necessary to set up some kind of procedure. First, if one purports to build 200 feet of fence something like 12 feet high, there must be a framework on which to hang, suspend, or attach the fencing itself, whatever the type: chicken wire, heavy or light hex netting, welded-wire fabric, chain link, or what have you. Thus speculation ensued as to the procurement and installation of the required fence posts, which could be wood, such as those at the West Side Tennis Court on Forest Street, or galvanized iron pipe, used at the Home-Ec courts, or something else. The decision was made in favor of iron pipe, and the search for this led immediately to the junk yards where used and discarded pipes of all kinds were then fairly plentiful.

Nineteen fifty was a time when antiquated steam-heating systems were becoming obsolete, frequently being thrown out in favor of hot-water systems in which smaller and lighter copper pipe is utilized as opposed to heavier black or galvanized. There was available considerable iron pipe of various sizes in local junk yards. Jim Pedace and this adviser were able to obtain the equivalent of about twenty-five lengths of this pipe, some two inches in diameter, some two and one-half inches, some one inch and a half, both black and galvanized—most of which had suffered little deterioration and therefore had good expectancy. Moreover, it was acquired free of charge. (The cost by today's standards of comparable new pipe would be around $2 per linear foot, which would amount to approximately $1,000 for posts alone, and just for backstops.)

Since the iron fence posts were to extend twelve feet above ground level, many not only had to be cut to proper length, but other shorter pieces had to be coupled together. In addition, it was important that the posts be set in adequate concrete footings, spaced and installed properly and perpendicularly. All of this represented a task far beyond the capability of any volunteer corps that could be recruited.

However, it happened that the city Water Department was on hand at the time, engaged in the installation of a water line under Mohegan Road from the artesian well in front of the clubhouse building to the courts. The department was headed, and for many years previously, by Mr. Jeremiah Kane. We have talked about some cooperative, class people thus far, but none finer than the late Superintendent Kane. Needless to say, he sent his men during some undemanding hours in the department to construct the fence. Welded-wire fabric, with one-by-two-inch rectangular mesh, was attached to the twelve-foot posts, spaced in line ten feet apart. There was no top rail.

Few additional tasks now remained before announcement of the opening of the tennis courts could be made. The net posts, donated by a local businessman and tennis enthusiast, Mr. Francis Plank, were installed promptly, and the lines laid down with dry lime in short order. Jim Pedace came up with nets he had uncovered somewhere in City Hall.

It was but a day or two less than three weeks since the meeting in the mayor's office, when the chairman of the Recreation Commission published the story of the two municipal courts in the *Norwich Bulletin*, announcing their opening. He paid tribute to all those who had participated in the task while proclaiming its consummation represented in many ways the finest cooperative civic effort that he could remember. Obviously, in light of the absence of resources, such an accomplishment could not have been achieved without the leadership and drive of Jim Pedace himself, who more than anyone was responsible for the amazing emergence of the facility in such a short time.

Play started in early August of that year, and, in fact, a tournament, the first ever held by the Recreation Department, took place in early fall. While we had our reservations as to how good the courts were at this stage, and while they hardly compared favorably with any facilities elsewhere, one thing was a virtual certainty, namely, that the tennis courts, although a far cry from the best around, were, in any case, the least expensive.

7

Emergence of the Stones and the Brain Trust

While characterization of the courts as the least expensive was probably appropriate, the terminology was woefully inadequate in respect to any realistic description of the tennis facility as it emerged after the first winter of existence in the spring of 1951. Any similarity between the area and playable clay tennis courts was lost upon the casual observer, and only the net posts and fences at the ends suggested the possibility of any connection even to knowledgeable tennis buffs. The place looked more like a cobblestone-and-pebble shallow beach at low tide.

It was a simple yet disheartening story, the winter's frost having heaved stones and fragmented rock from the integrated bank gravel to the surface. The south end was by far the worst, where the spring rains had washed out not only what little clay had been applied but also most of the substitute material Dick Pratt had helped roll in the year before. Dick, a Jim Pedace appointee, was the first supervisor and maintenance man of municipal tennis courts in Norwich's history, and one of the most dedicated. But neither Dick nor other municipal Recreation personnel was available in the spring of 1951, for the department functioned primarily during the summer months in those days. Thus it was up to the tennis players themselves to tackle the rocks and stones—that is, if they purported to play on the complex before Labor Day.

It was on Good Friday of that year that a small group was mobilized for what turned out to be an annual task. It is interesting that the start of the conditioning process on this sacred day became traditional, for Good Friday, whether early or late, is significant here in ways other than observance of the Crucifixion. First, it's a spring holiday, anxious tennis enthusiasts are available, and generally the winter's frost is by then out of the ground—a prerequisite to any conditioning procedure. But perhaps even more significant in the state of Connecticut at that time, all barrooms and cafés were closed on that day and thus one was able to retain the volunteer personnel for a longer period of time. The Deity apparently had an impact herein other than cloudbursts, earth slides, and associated storms, which, if memory serves accurately, never occurred on Good Friday in the decade of the 1950s.

The job of raking up the stones into piles and carrying them off in pails (wheelbarrows are not appropriate in the spring—ruts from the wheel are frequently discernible throughout much of the summer) is boring and frustrating. Understandably, productivity on Sundays fell far short of that on the Fridays before Easter, primarily because of the usual opportunity around midday for discussion as to alternatives, speculation as to possible easier procedures over relaxing beverage available at many convenient places opened for business at noon on the Sabbath. But, as in the case of any routine, there were exceptions to the scheduled exodus from the premises on Sunday afternoons in favor of places more conducive to philosophical reflection. One in particular occurred in the early 1950s when a couple of us elected to stick it out for a while longer, passing up the introductory part of the weekly session. The rock-and-stone-removal operation had not progressed to the point anticipated that day, the conference having started this time on the courts proper. Presently, after a pause for a back-straightening necessity and while looking south over the knoll of Reynolds Road, we observed an unusual sight, one noteworthy of mention.

The Norwich State Hospital, then as now, attracted and accepted many foreign doctors for their residency fulfillment in the field of psychiatry. Many of these young physicians understandably gravitated toward Norwich's municipal tennis courts evenings and weekends during summer months. Few had backgrounds in football, baseball, basketball, or golf, but nearly every one had some knowledge of and experience in tennis. We were pleased that facilities were available for them.

Dr. Eckard and Dr. Stein from Germany were two such young psychiatrists. Their participation in tennis, in a day when the idea of indoor courts in the area had started to no one's mind, was obviously limited to little over half the year when the gravel-and-clay integrated courts were playable. But Eckard and Stein had another exercise for the off season. Having pooled their resources to purchase an automobile, they would drive the three miles on weekends to the foot of Reynolds Road, park their jalopy, walk up the mile-long hill past the tennis courts, on through Mohegan Park, and eventually back to their car. In these days of the jogging enthusiasts such a routine would not be surprising, but at that time it was unusual if not implausible. Only Europeans would park a car at the bottom of a hill and walk up. And it wasn't because the auto couldn't make it.

We first noticed just the bobbing up and down of the heads of Eckard and Stein over the brow of Reynolds Road, but quickly they came into full view as they broke into a dead run. What was transpiring had struck home instantaneously, and they insisted upon immediate participation, on being part of the business at hand. Moreover, they worked without respite at an accelerated pace, like double time, and caused us to forget both fatigue and the weekly session.

Somewhat more was accomplished that afternoon than would have been at the conference table, it goes without saying. In fact, by dusk the major conditioning work was virtually complete, the courts ready to be rolled and lined. All of this represented one unforgettable and productive Sunday, at least the equal to that of any Good Friday—thanks to Dr. Eckard and Dr. Stein. They had concluded residency by conditioning time the ensuing year and had returned to Germany. Understandably, they did not show up to lend another great hand. But if they had we wouldn't have been surprised. Jet airplane travel was in its infancy by then.

Getting back to the spring of 1951, the exposed stones were eventually removed and the surface rolled with a twenty-four-inch hand roller. After imperfections such as holes, some like small craters, previous abodes of frost-heaved rock, were filled with clay, which could be spared at the extreme north end, the complex once again attained at least the appearance of an installation created for a specific purpose, namely, a facility for playing the game of tennis. The place became more recognizable as such after the lines were down and the nets were up.

It was at this point that the second year of tennis activity on municipal courts in Norwich became a reality. But for the tennis players, although few at the time, there were conditions and qualifications to that reality that suggested unmistakably that this activity would not be longlived unless additional improvements and embellishments somehow came to pass. Interminable Sunday afternoon conferences, while helpful and educational, could only point up the problems and requirements; they could not consummate them. Moreover, elongated discussion was superfluous, for the difficulties and limitations of the tennis court complex were glaringly obvious, and also numerous.

It is unimportant here to indicate priority in respect to the various inadequacies of Norwich's municipal courts in 1951; the following is just a simple run down. As stated previously, for sundry reasons the courts wound up with too much pitch from north to south, and one playing and hitting tennis balls from the south end not only had the impression of hitting uphill, but, in fact, he was. And there were additional facets to this situation that were even more discouraging; the pitch was so great that heavy rains had the effect of washing out the coveted clay from the premises, exposing more stones. In the long run, therefore, something had to be done about building up the south end, preferably with legitimate clay.

Something also had to be done about fences on the east and west sides. The one-hundred-foot backstops at the ends were simply inadequate for a battery of two courts properly spaced from each other; any angled or cross-court stroke that eluded the participants generally eluded the fence as well and wound up in the wooded underbrush, in which most players spent as much time looking for lost balls as they did on the courts. The problem was particularly severe to the west where, except in extended dry weather, a small stagnant pond prevailed. The gravel base brought in the year before did not extend far enough to prevent this. In addition, the surrounding underbrush was loaded with poison ivy. To be added to all this were the difficulties involved in the maintenance of unenclosed clay courts. Not only was it impossible to lock up the establishment when unplayable after rains (although for the many who go through, over, and under fences this is no deterrent), but also an enclosure was important in respect to other species, primarily dogs. Adjacent to this section of Mohegan Park, where new and expensive homes were then being built, more canines resided per human capita than at any place in the universe—and nearly all of the Great Dane, Saint Bernard, and German Shepherd variety. Their daily runs included the open courts whether playable or not, and some, large enough to take one's leg off, were captivated by the intermittent brushing and rolling procedure as well as the equipment itself—with which most were unfamiliar. The dogs followed and barked at both roller and drag brush just as they chased automobiles and, unlike the German psychiatrists, never lent a helping hand or offered assistance. In fact, the animals had little respect for the clay court surface as attested by the huge footprints, and they would do almost as much damage after rains as some impatient *Homo sapiens*. Moreover, their frequent presence had the effect of causing the precipitate flight of many prospective volunteer workers from the premises.

There are many reasons why little was accomplished in the summer of 1951 in the way of solving these problems. The one and important achievement was that of construction of the fence to the west—again by the Water Department with the cooperation of Superintendent Kane. Also, a four-foot door was installed in the southwest corner—thanks to the superintendent of Playgrounds, Anthony Kirker. While this critical addition on one side did little to protect the complex during and immediately following inclement weather, there was nonetheless a marked reduction in the number of cases of poison ivy infections. Perhaps if we had pleaded further, a fence to the east might well have become a reality also, but this would have been ill advised because of vague contemplation of eventually expanding the complex in that direction for tennis courts number three and four.

The early volunteer corps, or the "brain trust," which at that time included Ted Montgomery and Frank Aubrey, was a patient, imaginative group of men who didn't anticipate immediate solution of all the problems. Otherwise, they wouldn't be thinking in terms of courts three and four at this stage. Though Sunday afternoon consultations had been in vogue for some time with policy, activity, and program at the West Side court making up the entire agenda, the difficulties and challenges of the municipal courts now became new and exciting. Yet the boys were content to bide their time and enjoy the Sunday afternoon sessions with a sort of obscure expectation that the city courts would somehow work out in the end.

8

Appointment to Recreation Advisory Board

The comparative inactivity and lack of accomplishment in 1951 was related to considerations more broad in scope than municipal tennis courts, for the second year of the second half of the twentieth century was an historic one for Norwich. There had been an active citizens group in the community for some time, the moguls of which comprised a steering committee headed by Attorney Allyn L. Brown, Jr. The objective of the group was that of bringing about radical changes in the political and governmental structure of the city. There were all kinds of reasons and justifications for such an effort. After World War II an urgent need for reform in American cities was not only generally recognized, but at this point the movement itself was actually under way. Revamping of the administrative structure, centralization of administrative responsibility, and elimination of many separately elected independent officials were items long past due in municipalities that were becoming increasingly unable to discharge the functions and provide the necessary services commensurate with the demands of twentieth-century civilization. It was held by the citizens group that such reform was long past due in Norwich as well as any other place.

No attempt is made here to treat this development comprehensively, but it's appropriate to touch upon this significant period, certainly to the extent of its impact in the field of municipal recreation.

Some of the basic premises were that Norwich, now a bedroom town and not economically self-sufficient, simply hadn't kept pace with the times, that it was saddled with an inefficient, antiquated dual form of government—selectmen-town meeting for the entire area or town and an impossible jumble of a weak-mayor setup in the city, two governmental units superimposed on each other. For example, in Norwich in the second year of existence of its two municipal tennis courts, the city clerk, city treasurer, tax collector, the Water Board, city sheriffs, and members of the city council were elected along with the mayor in municipal elections. The city electorate also voted in town elections, in which they participated in the election of the town clerk and treasurer, the registrar of voters, the town tax collector, the Finance Board, assessors, the Board of Education, Board of Tax Review, constables, justices of the peace, as well as the selectmen. In the administrative organization of the city, the mayor appointed the Recreation Commission, the Park Commission, Gas and Electric Commission, the Finance Board, the Zoning Board, and the health officer, while the council appointed the assessors, the city engineer, corporation counsel, and three important commissions along with the associated department heads, in Police, Fire, and Street departments. The chief executive thus had limited direct control over city government.

Obviously such a structural setup contradicted virtually every organizational concept with respect to getting things done efficiently and reasonably. And after all, this is what municipal government is all about, for local government is responsible primarily for service-performing and regulatory functions, which vary widely in nature and character—from garbage collection to the maintenance of a municipal library, or to construction and maintenance of streets or even clay tennis courts. Fortunately, the Steering Committee was well aware of the reform movement in American cities and of the growing popularity of the council-manager form of government, conceived in large part by political scientists and championed by the International City Managers Association. The idea was that of replacing dual governmental hodgepodge with a symmetrical single administrative pyramid. Lines of control and responsibility from the grassroots personnel at the base would extend uniformly upward, from subordinate to superior, and converge at the apex in the person of the city manager, the appointed chief executive, trained and educated in the field of public administration. The manager, moreover, would be empowered to appoint the important department heads but on the basis of objective competitive examination, while the merit system would be in vogue for all city employees—somewhat of a departure from the system of appointment and hiring in line with political or other affiliation. It is easy to see, given proper structure by charter, all duplication and overlapping of function as well as the "gray areas" of responsibility would be eliminated under a single scientifically conceived municipal system.

Again, it is not for us here to treat the actual consummation of all this, the achievement of consolidation of town and city and the installation of the council-manager form of government in Norwich, except to say that it represented a remarkable effort by the citizens group (Citizens' Committee for Better Norwich Government) and the Steering Committee in particular, the chairman of which devoted six hours per day for at least a year to the difficult job of writing the new charter, which was adopted after two successful referendums set up by enabling legislation passed by the Connecticut General Assembly. Chairman Brown, along with attorney Guerson Silverberg and others must truly have been motivated, certainly with the conviction of making a contribution to human society in the Norwich area. One suspects that the young attorneys, having served in World War II, were, like the tennis players, in the right psychological frame of mind for the undertaking.

The new charter adopted in 1951 introducing the council-manager form of government beginning January 1952, a prodigious document spelling out, for example, sixty-three corporate powers of the city under Chapter III, irrevocably eradicated the old document, which had been "altered and patched up" for years without integrating new provisions with the old. Among the innovations, and the significant one here, was the creation of the Recreation Advisory Board, which replaced the previous Recreation Commission appointed by the "weak" mayor. The charter called for the administration of a recreation program under direct control of the city manager. The five-member advisory board, appointed by the city council for five-year overlapping terms, was to study the recreational facilities of the city and make recommendations to the city manager as to supervision, extensions, and improvements. Members of the board were to serve without compensation.

The new arrangement appeared to make a great deal of sense, a knowledgeable board advising a trained executive who would translate policy into quick and effective results. Obviously there would be no need for lateral maneuvers or approaches to independently elected department heads; there'd be no cause for commissioners or others to scrounge through junk yards for used and discarded iron pipe. Appropriate plans would be drawn for recommended and approved projects by the engineering section of the Public Works Department, and direct purchasing of materials by board members or lay citizens would be a thing of the past. The charter, in fact, provided for the creation of a Division of Purchase and Insurance headed by a purchasing agent under the Department of Finance. It would be the duty of the purchasing agent to contract and purchase, pursuant to rules and regulations established by ordinance, all supplies, materials, equipment, and contractual services required by any department or agency of the city—except the Board of Education. Such a horizontal auxiliary centralized purchasing agency servicing all departments and implementing across-the-board purchases at substantial savings made sense also—as did the purported function of the Department of Public Works, which would maintain virtually everything municipal from streets and buildings to parks and playgrounds. Why set up an independent maintenance staff and associated equipment for the Recreation Department, for example, when all this could be done by Public Works? Why not funnel the whole shebang under one trained and capable department?

For one who had been active for a couple of summers in an advisory capacity in connection with the random emergence of two municipal tennis courts, even though with unofficial status, the idea of actual official involvement under the promising new governmental setup became a matter of importance. Gaining appointment by the newly elected city council to the Recreation Advisory Board was both the proposition and the problem. One is inclined to believe he might be a natural for such an appointment on the basis of having worked gratuitously, but this is wishful thinking. First of all, there were then, as now, many people who devoted untold hours to programs and projects in the field of recreation and who were understandably and justifiably interested in an appointment. Moreover, the degree and extent of one's contribution is not the sole criterion in any event. Even though councilmen were elected on a nonpartisan basis—their names having been placed on the voting machines without party designation, with expectation that appointments, along with the myriad of other actions, would be more objective in nature—it is foolhardy to suppose that affiliations, contacts, interests, and associations are insignificant. Obviously, more than a few trips to Hartford or a week or two of picking rocks on tennis courts is of moment, particularly if such activity has been devoted exclusively to a poor relation.

Fortunately, however, a business associate, Leonard Partridge, was elected to that first council under the council-manager government, and he came through with flying colors—but it wasn't easy. An official advisory position in the field of recreation, however close the call, thus became a reality.

9

Additional Municipal Courts under New Government

It wasn't long after March 1952, the start of the first term on the board, when it became apparent that there were limitations and qualifications inherent in the new structural arrangement, and that things didn't always work out in actual practice exactly as envisioned. In fact, one frequently felt the unofficial advisory position under the weak-mayor system to be stronger than official advisory status under council-manager government. Paradoxically, while the previous function was for the most part truly advisory, the official one turned out to be operation "pick and shovel" primarily. Probably such a turn of events was to be expected, for the installation of managerial government called for by the new charter was difficult for Irving Beck, the first city manager. He had such a tremendous workload that recreation (clay tennis courts in particular) simply had to wait its belated turn. Then, too, the Recreation Department was a relatively minor one as attested by its operating budget. An organization meeting of the board was held, but nothing else transpired. Arnold Redgrave was elected chairman and what turned out to be lifelong associations with other board members, Dick Fontaine and Frank Delgado in particular, took place.

The young and capable manager, however, finally got around to paying some attention to his advisory board in early spring, about the time for conditioning of the tennis courts. Volunteers had by then completed the stone-removal process and the surface was ready to be rolled and lined. It was learned by the board that the Public Works Department, whose maintenance tasks were now all inclusive, had purchased a new lightweight power roller ideal among other uses for rolling clay courts. The manager directed Public Works to send the roller to the site along with an appropriate operator. There were two obvious routes through which this piece of equipment could be driven onto the tennis court surface: the open end to the east and the gate to the south. This board member, on hand theoretically for advisory purposes, strongly urged access via the gate at the south because of questionable muddy terrain at the open side in which the coveted roller might well get stuck. In retrospect, it probably would have been more fitting to advise the precarious route and the equipment might then have been directed through the gate. But knowledge of the workings of council-manager government was then elementary and unfortunate recommendations apparently made. Needless to say, the power roller, despite protracted insistence as to the hazards involved, did not make it to the courts for its first assignment. Continual revving of the motor only sunk the machine deeper into the quagmire and to the extent that it was necessary to haul it out with heavy tractors dispatched from headquarters. Not even the most optimistic observer could envisage any further use of the roller that day, for the gears and linkage were damaged and fouled with sufficient muck, mud, and clay as to preclude its use for some time—perhaps forever. At any rate, our final glimpse of the disabled roller, whose availability was anticipated with enthusiasm, occurred as it was dragged unceremoniously from the site.

There was no alternative now but to turn once again during evenings and weekends to timeworn hand-operated equipment, the manipulation of which was hardly advisory in nature. It was interesting shortly thereafter to take note of a release from the manager's office that appeared in the *Norwich Bulletin* to the effect that the tennis courts were conditioned and open for play at the earliest date in history. The article did not so state, but the implication was evident that such an accomplishment could have come to pass only under the new governmental setup. Moreover, it was not pointed out that the existence of the courts first came about way back in July 1950, nor that their history comprised one year and eight months of recorded time. Attainment of this significant achievement was tantamount only to surpassing the performance of one previous year.

Neither was the volunteer corps organized by a member of the advisory board, the same group that conditioned the courts in 1951 under the previous regime, mentioned in the release. It was becoming increasingly apparent, therefore, that considerable time would elapse before the concepts envisaged by the new charter would take place in actuality. The intent of the framers of the charger, brainchild of political scientists, creating an advisory board outside the administrative pyramid whose function was primarily that of establishing policy, contemplating implementation by administrative personnel, was both clear and encouraging. But it was also apparent that consummation of all this would not happen overnight, that the role of an advisory official would be of the pick-and-shovel variety for some time. It was not then observable, however, that this situation would remain essentially unchanged in the long run, for administrators were destined not only to participate in the policy-making process, but also actually to dominate in this area to a greater degree than anticipated, an understandable and inevitable development in a complex society. Political scientists had already noted that formulation of policy was "escaping legislative halls." Moreover, there's no hard and fast criterion as to what constitutes policy in municipalities anyway; it's "whatever the city council chooses to entertain preference about," according to one authority in local government. But even after such a determination by council there's frequently a "long row to hoe" before fruition. For an advisory board with far less power, despite appointment by the city fathers, the problems are compounded.

The charter provides for no place on the firing line for a member of the Recreation Advisory Board. He is powerless to prevent the demise of a power roller, for example, even though from a distance of ten feet from the fiasco. With no administrative authority it is generally inappropriate to approach line personnel laterally at any stratum of the pyramid. The only possibility is at the apex. And it would be futile to attempt salvage of a piece of equipment following the authorized route—seeking out the city manager (who probably would be in conference anyway), getting him to act, locating the proper subordinate with the appropriate "span of control," reaching down finally to the point where "advice" would be effective or even considered. Such procedure is productive only in creating resentment, and in any event is sufficiently circuitous and time consuming as to remove this avenue from consideration. One is better off to stay away from the scene and return with pick and shovel on weekends.

Since any viable contact with administrative personnel is therefore ruled out, it becomes necessary to explore other possibilities. One, of course, could call a meeting of the advisory board, but this generally was the long way around for a member interested in getting specific things done in the early years of council-manager government. In fact, with only a few exceptions, city managers have rarely met with the board or sought advice. And two of the seven chief executives Norwich has had in thirty years never once attended the sessions. Some members hadn't even met these gentlemen on any occasion and wouldn't have known the manager if they physically collided in or out of City Hall. Theoretically, meeting with the appointive director of Recreation satisfied all the requirements, since he represented the boss.

It is not the purpose here to cast reflections on any of the omnipotent seven but rather simply to point up the awkward situation. And it is not to say managers have been uninterested or that they have not stepped into the picture when situations called for administrative decisions—in respect to which the advisory board was generally left in the dark. Perhaps one of the reasons for reticence is that most had limited or no backgrounds on athletic fields and playgrounds, making it difficult to resolve problems, particularly in respect to those technical in nature. One manager, for example, when a budgetary problem arose, wanted the plate umpire handling league baseball teams to double up, acting both as umpire and official scorer. But city managers are not to be faulted herein, for the textbooks in public administration devote little space to municipal recreation, and few of the authors have backgrounds in city baseball or basketball leagues—nor have the majority of political scientists endeavored the construction of a municipal clay court tennis project without appropriate funds under either council-manager or weak- or strong-mayor governments. If they had, the weak-mayor system and direct department involvement would prevail hands down, for when municipal tennis courts are contemplated and constructed under the crossing-bridges-when-you-come-to-them procedure adopted for the first two in Norwich, the weak-mayor governmental setup is obviously the best. But it is equally obvious that such an approach to the building of a tennis facility, or anything comparable, is undesirable—just as the antiquated weak-mayor form of government for most cities is inadvisable, also. Recreation was then, and occasionally even today is, the only municipal department where this method was often employed.

Thus it is unfair and unintended here to downgrade the council-manager system, or even one structurally designed that recreational functions are to be carried out with the advice of a policy-making board with no administrative authority. What is implied, though, is that municipal recreation is probably a special case whose projects and programs are sufficiently diverse that type of government is relatively insignificant. (Perhaps this is not a profundity of the first rank, but applicable only to those municipalities that purport to construct and maintain clay tennis courts.)

To be considered here, also, is the traditional status of Recreation departments as the poor relation. While governmental activity in this area has grown in recent years to an unanticipated degree, it is still not one of the city's major functions—such as Education, Police, Fire, and Public Works. In addition, the nature of recreation in communities is unique in that the sum total of civic endeavor in this field far transcends that which governments directly administer. The schools, as well as Departments of Recreation, many organizations, churches, and service clubs of all kinds and description, are deeply involved. Thus the watchword is cooperation—emphasis on unmet needs and avoidance of duplication. Obviously, the total community effort includes involvement, work, and dedication of a great many people, far more than is immediately apparent when recreation is regarded in the broader sense. There's a lot more to it than leagues, play-offs, and tournaments in the traditional athletic games; activities and interests together with associated projects have become more numerous and intensified in the last few decades as are the necessary facets of departmental organizations for the programs—which vary from basketball to bridge.

It is understandably impossible to set up a comprehensive administrative structure that can encompass the entire community effort. Too many organizations are involved in the total picture, as well as so much dependence on volunteers—which is not to be discouraged. It could be said that recreational planning and activity when viewed in the large is a sort of pluralistic operation that defies superficial common denominators. The original concept of providing simply for leisure-time opportunities is inadequate these days. Suffice it to say here that the field of recreation in all of its aspects occupies a far larger place in human society than before, and necessarily so. In this complex age of multiplicity, people not only need outlets but also the chance to attain status and gain a sense of satisfaction from expenditure of energy and effort. This need now exists to a greater degree than ever.

But general recognition of all of this was not clearly apparent in the early 1950s, when an appointive recreation advisory official was a distant cousin. Yet his function was at least unique. The position of a commissioner or board member was substantially different from his counterpart in education or public utilities, whose assignment has actually approached that prescribed by charter. Board of Education members generally do not teach in the classroom, unlike advisory board members, who find themselves conditioning the infield, rolling the courts, and running the show. Nor does one observe a utilities commissioner climbing a telephone pole manipulating high-voltage power lines. Moreover, their budgetary documents were more clearly reflected in the actual programs and operations of the departments, and projects, then, as now, were not instituted or attempted, unlike clay tennis courts, without some plans and funding. Nor do many departments, except Recreation, often turn to business or industry, organizations or humanitarians for direct financial or other assistance.

When funds were appropriated in those days for capital recreation projects they were generally inadequate—particularly true in the early years of governmental participation in this area. One corporation counsel and occasional acting city manager once told this board member not to make requests for funds in connection with items or improvements unless the allocations approximated the cost of the jobs under consideration. It was necessary on frequent occasions for him to reject bids that were too far out of line. He was both correct and incorrect—that is, in respect to recreation, for, if adequate funds had been requested, chances of obtaining any appropriation whatsoever would have been nil. Better something than nothing, in other words. Thus financial assistance many times represented little more than a token endorsement. When for the Norwich fiscal year 1953-1954 budget, $1,000 was included in the city manager's requests, with the advice of the board, for tennis courts number three and four, members were not surprised that the figure was cut by $500. While allocation of such a ridiculous amount for a project of this magnitude probably indicated poor judgment and poor business on the part of both the board and the council, the action was nevertheless a significant one; namely, it was the first governmental appropriation for tennis in the history of the city of Norwich. In those days, when recreation was the poor relation among municipal functions and tennis a poor relation in recreation, such an action by council could be labeled as something of a milestone.

One may inquire as to why funds were asked for courts number three and four when the first two were far from finished. It was primarily because a two-court complex was not only inadequate as a central installation for a municipality of some thirty-odd thousand, but also that such a limited facility inclines to discourage interest and participation in the sport. Why get excited about the game, purchase a tennis racket, sneakers, and other attire when there's little or no chance to play—particularly at prime time. Therefore it was decided to proceed in this manner, leave the existing "side-hill" facility as is, and make whatever inroads possible toward an ultimate, acceptable battery of four tennis courts.

It was observed by this board member that the terrain to the east when stripped and leveled would approximate the grade of courts "one" and "two" and that the composition of the ground, a mixture of sandlike gravel and subloam, might well in itself serve as an adequate base, eliminating the necessity to truck in any bank gravel for the foundation. The idea was to obtain clay somewhere and integrate with, or trowel into, what was there, as was tried at the Forest Street court. Any other procedure, if the level of the two additional courts was to match the existing two, would necessitate removal of substantial material to allow for a base. The "bill of goods" was successfully sold to City Manager Beck and he forthwith sent the city grader to the area to proceed accordingly. The result not only lived up to expectations, but also improved the appearance of the whole place.

This operation was concluded at no expense to the department, and the $500 appropriation remained untouched and intact. Hopefully it would suffice for extension of the 12-foot fences at the north and south ends of purported courts "three" and "four." But, though the funds were now more imposing, far more than they would be in subsequent years, they were still inadequate for construction of a satisfactory fence. There were sufficient funds for purchase of the required 2,500 square feet of the same 1-inch-by-2-inch welded-wire fabric, and with something to spare, but not nearly enough for the footings and posts. It was the cost of the new black iron pipe that was again the stumbling block, and it prompted once more a return to the junk yards—this time under council-manager government. The used pipe so obtained gratuitously was, as previously, of different diameter and length, but having gone the route once before, it was successfully coupled and cut for proper height and installed by Public Works. The fencing job was completed subsequently, and as in the case of the 1950 construction three years earlier there was no top rail. The east end of the complex remained open, still providing easy access for both species *Homo sapiens* and species canine, whatever the conditions.

The next proposition was obviously that of making something comparable to a reasonable playing surface out of the existing terrain. One sticks his neck out, recommends procedures, fences built; it is incumbent upon him to come through somehow. The task would be complicated slightly by the absence of funds, since the first appropriation for tennis in Norwich's history was now nonexistent—and with no additional facilities to show for its expenditure. It therefore seemed imperative to come up with something that would suffice for tennis—at least temporarily. Speculation ensued, primarily at the regular Sunday afternoon sessions, and the decision was reached that possibly playable courts could be laid out on the area itself if properly prepared. Thus in midsummer 1953, volunteers, mostly members of the volunteer brain trust, started the business of raking out stones and grading the place by hand and "eye." Subsequent honing and rolling produced a surface that looked pretty good. But it wasn't as good as it looked by any means; the combination of fine sand and subsoil was simply not firm enough to withstand heavy traffic. However, we were able to improve the situation somewhat by introducing substantial amounts of calcium chloride, the use and advantages of which were by then fairly well known. Shortly thereafter net posts were installed, nets put up (all donated), and the least expensive of all tennis courts wherever opened for play. It was interesting to read about the opening in the *Norwich Bulletin* in the well-known column of Tom Winters, who referred to the "spanking new courts" at Mohegan Park.

The limitations, inadequacies, and imperfections of these makeshift new courts were not lost on the volunteers of the brain trust, however, and when the Sunday afternoon sessions resumed in early summer of 1954 the proposition of improving the surface of courts "three" and "four" was high on the agenda. One imaginative member of the group came up with what he thought to be a sure-fire solution to the problem, but not until well along with the third fifteen-cent beer. Since the surface required firmness and solidification, why not broadcast straight dry Portland cement directly from the bag after scarifying the ground lightly? The more he thought about it, the more the certainty. Ultimate undeniable assurance was advanced after expenditure of another thirty cents. The scientific breakthrough was not only heralded by the brain trust and adopted for courts "three" and "four," but was envisioned as an innovation that would solve similar problems faced by municipalities nationwide—after expenditure of thirty more cents.

Though attainment of desired solidification of the surface was accomplished beyond question, it turned out that the scientist of the brain trust should have had fewer rounds. Firmness was established all right, but the inescapable presence of granular material on top of the playing surface made for conditions more slippery than the Home-Ec courts ever were. Playing tennis on the courts was hazardous and even dangerous, and participants, including many of the brain trust, frequently sprained ankles or went over the proverbial "tea kettle" and "bandbox." Something obviously had to be done about the situation and another approach was in order. A decision was made at the next meeting of the founding forefathers; namely, obtain some real clay somehow and integrate with, or trowel into, the surface as originally planned.

City Manager Beck agreed to send a Public Works truck, capacity of five cubic yards, to a Middletown brickyard, charging the clay to our Buildings and Grounds maintenance account. One truckload doesn't seem like much and it sure is a far cry from the barest minimum requirement for two courts (amounting to an application of less than one-eighth of an inch), but brickyard clay is very rich and goes farther than one might think—since it integrates with and stiffens appropriate other material. Such a small amount, however, can improve a surface only temporarily, and this would be the case here after introduction of the clay (mostly by hand trowels) had been accomplished by the brain trust in a few tough work sessions.

Yet the "spanking new courts" now were playing very much better, were no longer too slippery and dangerous, and in later summer of that year, 1954, the Fourth Annual Norwich Tennis Tournament took place—for the first time on four courts. (It's another matter of interest that this tournament was won by nationally known Alphonso Smith, who at the time was the number-two ranking senior tennis player, age forty-five and over, in the nation. He happened to be in the area—at General Dynamics in Groton doing liaison work for the U.S. Navy. Alphonso has remarkable credentials. In 1924 he was the National Boys champion, age sixteen and under, and in 1964 he won the first U.S. Senior-Senior Tournament, age fifty-five and over, in Las Vegas. Two national titles separated in time by forty years. We were happy he was able to play here on our makeshift municipal courts.)

Despite the progress made and success of programs, clinics, and tournaments, it was important, nevertheless, for the brain trust to assess these gains objectively and to face up to the reality of the accomplishments. The truth of the situation was both obvious and difficult to acknowledge, namely, that the courts were poor, in fact almost a hypocrisy. Perhaps they weren't quite that bad, assuming proper maintenance, but there was nothing resembling any permanence about them. And all appraisals indicated that Norwich's municipal clay courts would not be long for this world short of a major operation. Witness the piecemeal operations on courts "three" and "four," and the clayless south ends of courts "one" and "two," and the fence posts from the junk yards with no top rail.

All of this comprised the subject matter for the Sunday afternoon sessions in the fall of 1954, after the tournament won by Alphonso Smith. It was not difficult to conceive of the major operation with number-one priority, but it was well outside the scope of the imagination to envisage any way to attain its consummation. What was required was merely about 250 cubic yards of good clay, which would be utilized to build up the south ends of the first two and provide a legitimate surface for the second two courts. We could not contemplate another lucky break as in the case of the Phoenix Mutual contractor in Hartford; we couldn't approach department heads or selectmen directly as under the weak-mayor regime; and we would have been run out of town if we asked for an adequate appropriation through normal channels. Too many justifiable and competing interests existed in Recreation seeking limited available funds, and too many unfinished projects were clearly apparent in areas other than tennis for one to get away with this, or even try.

10

Clay from Coventry

In view of the formidable, apparently insurmountable difficulties, primarily the acquisition of clay in large volume, the stalwarts of the brain trust understandably became frustrated for a while that fall, and a sense of despair permeated the Sunday afternoon sessions. The manpower was on hand, ready to proceed with pick and shovel, but there was no material to work with—nothing appropriate to distribute over the improvised surface of the municipal courts. But comparable situations had been faced before and there was faith that something progressive would transpire soon. It did.

It was learned about this time that the University of Connecticut was then in the process of building a nine-court complex on its campus, utilizing clay from a deposit located on the farm of the late Sterling Mott in Coventry, which is four miles north of Willimantic and a comparable distance from the university at Storrs. Ramifications as to how this source was found, or how the contractor learned of its existence, are not known here, but it could easily be assumed that the clay was acceptable in quality, that it obviously passed required tests, and that it must have been available in substantial quantity if used for the surface of nine courts—whereupon this advisory board member immediately sought consultation with Mr. Mott.

The conference was long, educational, constructive, and interesting. The clay was of excellent quality for tennis courts, not as rich as that from brickyards and easier to handle. But there was a major qualification; it was full of stones both large and small. The

University of Connecticut contractor had rigged up a contraption for screening the clay, and while Mr. Mott charged a very nominal price for the material, the cost after processing and screening came to about nine dollars per cubic yard. It is easy to see that such a procedure was an impossibility for a municipality without contractor or funds. Yet conversation continued and Sterling Mott was briefed in due course as to the problem at the Norwich tennis complex. Since a government recreational department was involved, he subsequently said, "You can have the clay free of charge if you want to take stones and all." It was a deal, he was told, provided arrangements for loading and trucking could be made. The enthusiastic members of the brain trust could throw out the stones by hand. All the gentleman farmer would require was that his terrain, after being chewed up and stripped, be restored in reasonable condition. What a great guy!

The obvious next consultation was in City Hall with Manager Irving Beck, a University of Connecticut graduate. There was no way both loading equipment and trucks could be sent twenty-odd miles to the Sterling Mott farm, but Public Works could allocate four city dump trucks for one day, provided adequate notice was given. The cooperative city manager was then asked if the budget could stand retainment of a contractor with a steam shovel, perhaps the one who loaded for the University of Connecticut tennis court contractor. "See what you come up with and we'll go from there," he responded. Another get-together was arranged with Mr. Mott, who came through with all the desired information: name, address, and telephone number of an Eagleville, Connecticut, trucking firm up the road from Coventry a few miles on Route 32. The Eagleville contractor agreed to return his steam shovel to Mott's clay bed for one day along with some of his own trucks. The four Public Works trucks would not be able to keep his loading equipment busy nor deliver the required volume in an eight-hour stretch.

Back at City Hall the city manager, after briefing as to procedure and after being reminded the clay was free of charge, gave the go-ahead. Thus came to pass another extralegal exercise, an advisory board member negotiating directly with contractors in the name of the city, as under the weak-mayor system. (Where municipal clay tennis courts are involved, it is clear that form of government is irrelevant.) It was thought appropriate to spell out the impending transaction to the chairman of the advisory board, the late Arnold Redgrave, who acquiesced without hesitation, but there were no further substantiations or assurances endeavored. The show was clearly on the road. And the road was Route 32.

A considerable part of the next day was spent in making arrangements for the transportation of the clay the day following. There was a compulsion to work fast and a sense of urgency about the whole thing, for such a precipitate action might not prove to be very popular and might well be open to criticism. Perhaps a meeting should have been called, certainly plans should have been submitted for approval, and so on. But it was felt there'd be no surer way to kill the project than taking that avenue. Moreover, the clay bed was exposed, the trucking firm was fresh off its University of Connecticut assignment, and there was no better time for Sterling Mott.

In setting up the arrangements there were some difficulties in coordination and timing that had to be resolved. The city drivers knew where the tennis courts were, the Eagleville truckers were well familiar with the area of the source at Mott's farm in Coventry, but neither knew of both or how to get there. Also, the original idea of leading the city trucks to Coventry and the others back to the tennis courts had to be discarded. The Eagleville steam shovel contractor was an "early bird" who started operations at 6:00 A.M., while the Public Works trucks could not leave the garage before 8:00 A.M. But this advisory board member conceived of a foolproof plan that would solve this elementary problem as follows: simply load the Eagleville trucks in the early hours and send them down Route 32 toward Norwich. The vehicles loaded with clay would be easily identified by one on the lookout who would then take the lead to Mohegan Park. They would be ready to return to Coventry around 8:00 A.M. and the Public Works trucks could follow. Simple enough.

One-fifth of the advisory board was up and ready to go shortly after 5:00 A.M. on that nippy but pleasant October morning in 1954 for the first assignment, that of locating and leading the Eagleville trucks to the municipal courts. It was an enjoyable cruise at the beginning of this eventful day on Route 32, this time in a brand-new Chevrolet convertible with less than one hundred miles of highway experience—the driver by then having discarded long since the junk contraption maneuvered to Asylum Avenue four years earlier. Things were totally different now. First, we were going to get a very substantial volume of clay this time around and, second, infallible plans had been made accordingly. Thus it was relaxing and also appropriate to be driving a new car under such circumstances with serenity and confidence, for presently the Eagleville trucks, laden with the coveted clay, would be coming into view approaching Norwich, Connecticut.

However, when by 7:30 A.M. no trucks had been observed, apprehension began replacing calm and serenity, and by 8:00 A.M. had completely superseded. Route 32 was soon abandoned and contact made with the Public Works trucks, which had just arrived at Mohegan Park. After momentary deliberation they were directed to proceed north on "32" toward Willimantic and wait at the underpass just before entering the city proper—that is, if the Chevrolet convertible had not overtaken the trucks by then. To stray too far north at this time would be foolish since at any moment the Eagleville trucks might show, and perhaps in time for the convertible to catch up with the city trucks prior to their stopping point. But there was a time limit, for it would be unwise to leave the trucks outside Willimantic all morning. About 8:30 A.M. it was decided to take off for that city and lead the Norwich vehicles to Sterling Mott's farm. And take off that Chevrolet did. Seldom has a new automobile been broken in at such an accelerated pace. As the flight proceeded north on Route 32 it was hoped for the first time in over three hours that no Eagleville trucks would come into view for a while. But when streaking through the lowlands of Franklin, something else did, but not for long.

Apparently the unusual sight of a new car flying by with wheels barely in contact with the highway caused the departure of a good-sized pheasant from its habitat in some heavy foliage beside the road. The exodus across Route 32 elected by the pheasant smack in the path of the convertible was unfortunate, as its protoplasm was disintegrated and splattered into a thousand million entities of molecules—through the grill, the radiator, and over the windshield—all of which made for a reduction in speed down to about eighteen miles per hour, the recommended rate set forth by the pre-Wimbledon progenitor in the time of the heyday of Big Bill Tilden and Little Bill Johnston in the 1920s. (Twenty m.p.h. was a shade too fast.)

There was no choice except to proceed at the pater's suggested rate to Carboni's gas station where the new Chevrolet was hosed down. A more reasonable flight ensued for the remainder of the trip to the underpass at Willimantic where the four city trucks were parked, the drivers in sedentary repose. No Eagleville trucks had appeared as of this point. However, as the convertible led the Public Works vehicles through the center of the thread-mill city, first one and then another of the overdue conveyances were observed proceeding south through heavy traffic. It couldn't have happened at a more unfortunate place, and thus the Chevrolet, unable to make contact, was committed to continue leadership of the entourage to the Mott farm, and at a pace reduced to the maximum speed of the slowest municipal truck. The four miles to Coventry seemed interminable.

After arrival at long last at the clay-bed site and after momentary exchanges with Sterling Mott and the steam shovel operator, who explained that an unanticipated breakdown had altered his timetable, the Chevrolet convertible forthwith took off on its next flight to Norwich and Mohegan Park. No flying objects were encountered on the return trip, which was negotiated at a rate of speed not to be recorded here. It is enough to say that while for an advisory board member the operation itself was probably *extra*legal all along, according to charter, it was also *il*legal on Route 32.

The whereabouts of the Eagleville trucks was unknown, of course, but happily one was observed parked adjacent to Chelsea Parade as the Chevy slowed for landing during approach to good old Norwich. The others had elected to seek out the tennis courts, inquire from police and others, but in the fall of 1954 relatively few knew of the existence of such a complex—let alone how to direct anybody to it. Soon, however, all of the long-sought trucks were corralled, one having been located in the very center of the city at

Franklin Square where the driver fortunately did not dump his load, and all were eventually directed to the municipal courts. Now, finally, both the municipal trucks and those of the Eagleville contractor knew all they needed to know, as did the Chevrolet convertible, which, having started its life experience earlier that day as a neophyte, emerged after just a few hours a seasoned veteran.

11

Four Tennis Courts Completed

The two-hundred-odd cubic yards of clay lay dormant in about fifty closely joined heaps throughout the 1954-1955 winter. There was nothing aesthetic about it either subjectively or objectively, although the mass looked better when covered with snow. In fact, its presence on courts "three" and "four" made little sense, for the muck and stones from Coventry seemed to have no relation or potential in respect to a playable tennis court surface. It was sometimes referred to as this board member's pile of "material"—paraphrased generally in four-letter words. Moreover, there were occasional overtones hinting that acquisition of the stuff was no doubt illegal. And it was further embarrassing when a few members of the brain trust became skeptical. But the overriding fact was the presence of the piles, whatever the descriptive phraseology—an irreversible fait accompli. And not even the most vehement critic suggested return of the implausible bulk to Mott's farm in Coventry.

In light of this background it was imperative for what was left of the brain trust to tackle the mess at the earliest date possible in the spring of 1955. The job would be endeavored this time directly by the individual responsible, and with no solicitation of help from City Hall. Public Works would be too busy on the streets and highways at that time anyway, and even if available, their procedure might well begin by bulldozing the premises. Two municipal departments were helpful, however, but in an unofficial and extracurricular capacity. Neither Richard Korenkiewicz, faculty member in Education, nor Stanley M. Bierylo, director of Welfare, both tennis enthusiasts, withdrew support. Not only did they offer encouragement verbally, but actually pitched in manually and physically—after hours on weekdays and many hours on weekends. It was fitting that such assistance was forthcoming, for Education, Welfare, and Recreation, far from being diametrically opposed, are really on the same side of the fence, working toward common objectives. Ironically and incongruously, the director of Welfare had been reprimanded and blasted by tennis-playing citizens on more than one occasion because of alleged frequent poor playing conditions. Apparently the director worked so consistently on weekends that some of the populace assumed he was an employee of the Department of Recreation rather than Welfare. But Stan rolled with the punches, did not attempt an explanation, and took it all philosophically without blinking an eye.

The first stage of the job, distributing the two hundred or so cubic yards of clay as evenly as possible, consisted of two major operations tackled concurrently. It was necessary to throw out the stones as well as apply the material. Obviously this gigantic assignment was a backbreaker, which was endeavored for the most part without tools or equipment—except for the wood-handled iron pick. The piles of clay broke into good-sized chunks exposing stones of various sizes. Almost none was so large that it couldn't be carried away by hand, and the remaining chunks of clay could be chopped down to negotiable dimensions and handled similarly. Distribution of the clay over the south ends of courts "one" and "two" and the entire surface of "three" and "four" proceeded slowly in the presence of almost no one. Occasionally an inquisitive member of the brain trust would show up, but of a sudden was reminded of an urgent commitment elsewhere. Others arrived just before lunch or dinner where punctuality was the inescapable watchword. One indicated more allegiance than previously observed to his sanctum of worship, his consistent attendance automatically assumed. And another apparently did more preparatory work on the Sabbath for the forthcoming week than heretofore realized.

The stone-removal-and-distribution-of-clay procedure continued, however, and the place soon came gradually to resemble a freshly plowed field. Further progress toward transformation of the fifty piles to reasonably level clay tennis courts was achieved both by Mother Nature, in the form of periodic heavy rains, and a couple of rugged iron rakes. And even though the surface was crude and rough, it was a profound relief to observe at long last some real clay on the south ends of courts "one" and "two." Yet there was still a long way to go before the facilities could be opened for play. But at precisely this point in time invaluable assistance came from an unexpected source.

On an earlier page something of the story of acquisition by the city of this section of Mohegan Park, now known as Recreation Field, was mentioned—in connection with the unfinished Works Progress Administration project prior to World War II. The pertinent qualification in the transfer of ownership by the Norwich Free Academy to the city relates to the provision in the deed whereby the academy would be guaranteed use of the facilities during the academic year. Such an arrangement made a great deal of sense then, and even more so today. There would never be adequate space adjacent to the school itself for the fields required for participation in modern interscholastic athletic programs. In previous days the one field behind the main building had to suffice for the outdoor physical education and athletic programs in entirety. Football, baseball, track, and all appropriate curricular activities for students transpired on the same ancient site. It goes without saying that the multipurpose field took quite a beating, and consequently could never be a first-class area for any single sport or function. For many years now, however, Norwich Free Academy teams have been using the facilities at Recreation Field, both for practice and interscholastic events themselves. The football team, unlike baseball, continues to play its games on the field at the NFA campus, but training and preparation throughout the week takes place at the park. And as in the case of baseball, the entire interscholastic tennis program (boys in the spring and girls in the fall) is run on the city courts. Except for the fall schedule for girls, now in full bloom, this arrangement was in vogue even in 1955 when Richard "Doc" Jensen was the tennis coach—therefore the urgency that spring to complete the difficult resurfacing job at hand.

Since joint use of the facilities is involved there have been occasional visitations over the years to Recreation Field by top administrative officials from the Norwich Free Academy. Happily, one such visit occurred at this critical time in the person of the late Paul Bradlaw, treasurer of the school, business manager, teacher, printer, gentleman and friend. He stayed for some time at the tennis courts, observing the manual operation, and to such length that he was very probably late for dinner. (Apparently his busy schedule was slightly more flexible than that of certain members of the brain trust.) Before leaving, however, he had not only studied the situation, but could see that a real boost would be very much in order. And prior to departure he offered to send landscaper Lindy Hildebrand, retained by NFA for sundry maintenance jobs, to the courts at the school's expense. The proposition was obviously accepted instantaneously, and Hildebrand, thanks to Paul Bradlaw, arrived by mid-morning the following day. Previously in this writing, accolades have been made justifiably and intentionally in behalf of others. It's time now to say something about Paul. Few more dedicated and cooperative individuals have lived and worked in any community on this planet than the long-time business manager. Small wonder that the manual training building where this gentleman spent a great portion of his life is known now, and will be so long as civilization and the Norwich Free Academy survive, as the Bradlaw Building.

Fortunately, distribution of the clay over the area had reached the point where Hildebrand's grading equipment could be used effectively. And after something like six hours a very satisfactory surface for a four-court tennis complex was a reality. The remaining tasks, such as rolling and lining the courts, were comparatively easy. Neither Mr. Bradlaw, Mr. Hildebrand, nor this advisory board member could then foresee the extent of the activity that would ultimately transpire on the clay from Sterling Mott's farm. That by 1980 over thirty major New England tournaments, sanctioned by the United States Lawn Tennis Association, would have been held on those courts, that for the next twenty-five years Norwich Free Academy tennis teams would have practiced and played interscholastic matches there, were ultimate eventualities that were then beyond a remote figment of the imagination—even of the most visionary of the brain trust, no matter the number of rounds of libation. It is profoundly hoped that the facility will continue to be so utilized, and for more than just another quarter of a century.

But history cannot be written in advance of human experience. And no one really knows what the experience will turn out to be—in the short or long term. The beginning of the ninth decade of the twentieth century is far different from the start of the sixth when Jim Pedace and this board member first viewed the prospective site for tennis courts in Mohegan Park. Any half of one day in the 1980s would be sufficient time for a modern giant Caterpillar dozer to obliterate the area where the courts reside, wiping out thirty years of pick-and-shovel effort. And for one reason or another, such an occurrence could take place, to say nothing of other possibilities. It is optimistically assumed here, however, that such will not be the case and that something of the story of the remaining quarter century, 1955 to 1980, may add a small increment of insurance for the survival of the courts. Some knowledge of even such an infinitesimal segment of history may stay the hand of possible future hard court advocates.

12

Calcium Chloride and Painted Lines

In the preceding chapter we were in the spring of 1955 when Lindy Hildebrand and his men had leveled and honed the surface of the courts very satisfactorily. It was an impressive-looking area now with an adequate layer of clay. Thanks to Sterling Mott and the Phoenix Mutual contractor, the city of Norwich was the recipient of all that clay for the sum of zero dollars and zero cents. A moderate and reasonable charge for trucking represented the only expenditure. But once again the now rejuvenated brain trust had to face up to actuality. There was still no fence at the east end of the complex, there was no top rail connecting the various sized posts from the junk yards, very little was known about suitable top dressing, the water supply was very inadequate, and we continued to line the courts with dry lime. The twenty-five years from 1955 to 1980 saw some, but by no means all, of these problems solved. We'll take them one at a time.

In late summer of 1955 a significant and almost life-transforming suggestion came from the late Saul Shenfield of New London. Saul, a frequent winner of eastern Connecticut events, former New London city champion and New England ranking player, was in town for our annual tournament. He could readily observe the difficulties involved in the unending application of the dry lime for lining the courts—which, apart from the constant labor entailed, was unsatisfactory from the beginning. The lime scatters and blows all over the place and washes away after rains. In addition, the Recreation

Department could afford to retain personnel for court operations only in the summer months. (Anthony Tramontozzi and Larry Coletti, then college students and now well-known surgeons, were the applicators in those days.) None of this was lost upon Saul Shenfield who came up with the solution to our problem. It was linseed oil and traffic paint.

Whether this system of laying down lines for tennis courts was deliberately conceived or was an accidental discovery is not known here, but it is true that raw linseed oil, available in one-gallon cans at most hardware or paint stores, will solidify virtually any type of terrestrial ground—including clay. A firm base thus can be established for subsequent application of traffic paint. Saul had observed this procedure in the city of New Haven where he frequently played tennis. One unsubstantiated story is that a workman accidentally spilled some linseed oil on their municipal courts, later noticing the solidification after the oil had dried. Whatever the case, this system of lining tennis courts was used at certain locations for a while—even at sophisticated places such as the New Haven Lawn Club and Wentworth-by-the-Sea in Newcastle, New Hampshire. While there are many reasons why the innovation was relatively shortlived elsewhere, it has proven a uniquely advantageous method for the special circumstances at the municipal courts in Norwich, Connecticut, where painted lines have predominated now for one quarter of a hundred years. More of the linseed oil and traffic paint story will be discussed later on; suffice it to say here that, had the procedure not been adopted, maintenance of these and other facilities in the area probably would have been impossible.

The rest of the items on the agenda of the brain trust were not solved as readily, except for the fence at the east. Installation of a barrier at this side of the rectangle was accomplished the ensuing year under the regime of Jay Etlinger, Norwich's second city manager. It was an easy "bill of goods" to sell—particularly at a time when the emergence of a legitimate facility was clearly apparent. Only a couple of appointments with the manager were required to attain another go-ahead from City Hall. Again, extralegal procedure was in store for this board member who one more time engaged a contractor directly—the late Henry Lebejko. Extralegal or not, it was another profound relief to observe at long last a complete enclosure and to be able to lock the complex when unplayable. Moreover, consummation of the east fence project was accomplished in this case without the usual search through junk yards, for Jay not only authorized the purchase of new iron pipe, but also in standard lengths of identical diameter. Consistency and uniformity was maintained, too, since there was no provision for a top rail.

The brain trust was happy with the fait accompli, however, and though the unaesthetic fence was not perfect, it served the basic purpose of preserving the courts when weather conditions precluded play. Moreover, almost no one took much note of the tennis court fence, anyway; it was painted green and thus blended with the Mohegan Park foliage on the north, south, and west sides. Yet a top rail has significance other than appearance and durability, for if shade curtains or wind screens are contemplated, such a connector from post to post is indispensable. We couldn't know in 1955 that it would be well over a decade before installation of either top rail or shade curtains would come to pass, and therefore this story will wait for a subsequent page.

It didn't require ten years to solve the top-dressing problem, however. All members of the brain trust were not only aware of the desirability of a covering over the surface, but many had observed its consistent use at facilities elsewhere while playing the New England circuit. Clay, whether from Coventry, Asylum Avenue, brickyards, or wherever, needs some kind of granular embellishment on top—particularly appropriate in humid weather or after rains when the courts would otherwise be too greasy and slippery. And without it the tennis balls will frequently discolor and gain in weight. While none of this was lost upon the intelligentsia, the boys were frustrated nonetheless. The need was clearly recognized, volunteer manpower for application was available, but there was no resources to obtain the top dressing itself, namely, that indispensable commodity that comes first—that is, cash. It would be at least a year or two before funds would be available in the Recreation budget for purchase and trucking of the excellent granular slate from Granville, New York. (Redkote is the technical name of the product we decided upon.) But the whole story was soon known by a business executive and humanitarian, Irving Castle, president of Lehigh Petroleum, who was close to the situation. The slate arrived upon the scene in time for our first sanctioned tournament in 1956. Earlier that year, the Norwich Tennis Association was organized and membership in the United States Lawn Tennis Association had been established.

The quarter century 1955 to 1980 did not see the consummation of the other aforementioned inadequacy, however. And this problem may not be solved by the end of two and a half more decades—by 2005. Reference is, of course, made to the water supply. While the city of Norwich is blessed with relatively limitless resources herein, the water mains, nonetheless, do not extend up the mile-long Reynolds Road hill to Recreation Field. Apparently, expensive pumping stations would be required, the cost of which was understandably out of proportion in respect to prospective usage. And even the most rabid of the brain trust would admit to the folly of a colossal expenditure simply for the purpose of watering clay tennis courts.

This is not to say that water in our fine Recreation Building, at the baseball field or the tennis courts, is nonexistent. On the contrary, the artesian well in front of the building, age approximately forty-five years, provides the finest drinking water available almost anywhere—as attested by the frequent visits of hundreds of citizenry who return home laden with filled containers. For many the water is clearly preferable to that from the reservoirs. But it's the quantity rather than the quality of the water that is pertinent here. Pressure and volume, together with the antiquated and piecemeal underground piping structure, are such as to comprise a system adequate for drinking fountains and bathroom and kitchen facilities only. Satisfactory watering of the tennis courts or the baseball fields under the present arrangement is an impossibility. And, even assuming sufficient quantity, these difficulties would be only slightly alleviated because of limited outlets. There's an inch and a quarter pipeline under Mohegan Road from Recreation Building to the tennis complex, but no piping under the courts proper. Any type of sprinkler system is therefore ruled out. Some efforts have been made to improve the situation, such as the installation of an additional outlet adjacent to the south fence (making a grand total of two outlets now) and some upgrading of the mechanics of the artesian well itself. Had not these improvements been made, reasonable maintenance of our facilities throughout the quarter century would have been more difficult.

One looks back in retrospect after thirty years in official, though "advisory," capacity in Recreation and is appalled at his failure to solve the water supply problem on a satisfactory permanent basis. Particularly in the second half of the twentieth century when technology, equipment, and know-how are such that this and similar problems should be readily solvable. True, the proposition here involves plumbing, electrical, volume, pressure, maintenance, and surveillance considerations. True, also, that consummation could not have been achieved in this case by volunteers during evenings and weekends with pick and shovel. It is easy to enumerate the alibis, as for example preoccupation with the many and difficult tasks in construction of a four-court (later, six-) tennis complex with virtually no planning or funding. But there's no adequate excuse for failure herein. After all, Kelly Junior High School is a mere 200 yards away; built subsequent to the tennis courts, it has its own plentiful water source independent from the city's reservoirs. The artesian well at the school is not only sufficient to fulfill all the requirements at the junior high but it also provides the water necessary to run the sprinkler system at the new soccer field across the road at Mahan Drive. It's the only available source for the field.

Thus the idea of a new well in the area for the purpose of supplying both the tennis courts and the baseball fields should not be dismissed, nor should the proposition of reconstructing the existing well near Recreation Building, which conceivably could be upgraded to the point required to do the whole job. If a satisfactory source can materialize at Kelly Junior High School, why not at Recreation Field? Unfortunately, it is not possible to dig an artesian well with pick and shovel, or brain trust enthusiasts would have tackled the project long ago.

This omission in accomplishment has both complicated the task of maintaining the tennis courts throughout the thirty-year period and caused the emergence of some routines that are positively anachronistic—at least in appearance. The antediluvian exercises have dealt with the procurement and application of the indispensable calcium chloride. Until nearly the end of the third quarter of the century, in the early 1970s, the coffers in annual Recreation budgets were always inadequate for purchase of any of the chloride whatsoever. Its availability came about in various ways, some contributed by tennis players, some by business concerns (Cash Home Center, for example), and occasionally fairly substantial amounts charged to a personal account. But application of the calcium has been even more difficult than its obtainment. While the commodity may be broadcast in flake form direct from the bag by hand or shovel, or applied more evenly utilizing a lawn spreader, effective introduction of the salt is here contingent on favorable weather conditions. The optimum time for spreading calcium chloride in this manner is just prior to nightfall when atmospheric moisture, which provides the necessary dissolving agent, is at its height. However, volunteer personnel are seldom available at this hour, the courts are usually still in use (some endeavor play in almost total darkness), and municipal maintenance personnel have long since departed, having completed their daily work schedule at 4:00 P.M..

Yet, assuming the presence of both calcium chloride and the requisite manpower, late-evening application is not always effective, particularly for Norwich's sprinklerless clay courts, which frequently become dry to the point that deeper penetration of the chemical is essential. The tennis facilities are the victim or beneficiary, invariably the former, of whatever the pattern of precipitation turns out to be. Brain trust stalwarts know from experience that protracted dry spells occur most often the fortnight prior to sanctioned tournaments. They are certain that the rains will come eventually, but not until after the competition begins, and in the form of cloudbursts—inevitably during the semifinals and finals.

It has been incumbent upon the brain trust to adjust to the situation, first to condition the dry courts prior to tournament play, then cope with the downpours later on. During the middle 1950s the men would occasionally fail on this score. In fact, one of the participants approached this advisory board member after a match he had played in an early tournament and stated bluntly that court number "two" was the worst he had ever played on. No doubt he would have been less vehement had he not lost the match. Also, during this period it was not uncommon that the president of the Thames Valley Tennis League would relay complaints from some of the players as to the condition of the courts—as a rule from members of the losing team. These unsought communications did not appreciably augment the morale of the hard-working brain trust.

But the dedicated stalwarts had to face up to the legitimacy of the complaints, nonetheless, for playing in clouds of clay dust is unenjoyable, whether winner or loser. Thus speculation ensued, primarily as to how to attain a deeper penetration of the calcium chloride. All this resulted in a unique system conceived by the group, which has been perfected to a limited degree over the years. And though nineteenth-century in administration and procedure, it has worked satisfactorily and with reasonable dispatch. The process is simply that of applying calcium chloride in solution, dissolving it first in the water from the artesian well, which is just about adequate for this purpose.

In the beginning, this tennis-court-salvaging operation, which arbitrarily can be pursued at any time of day, high noon or dusk, was negotiated with ten-quart plastic sprinklers, the kind one uses to water flowers. But this approach to an area of approximately 25,000 square feet could not even be classified as nineteenth-century—closer actually to the Dark Ages. The brain trust, however, had to face up to the requirements of the 1950s and forthwith applied their collective intellects and imagination accordingly, eventually coming up with a unique procedure. It was a pail-slinging operation.

The water source from the outlet near the south fence is sufficient to keep one man busy broadcasting water from a ten- or twelve-quart pail. Two such containers would be needed if the water was allowed to run continuously, one being filled while the other was carried away to be applied. Obviously, if calcium chloride is to be dissolved first, more than one individual would be required for the job—that is, if the faucet is to be left open constantly. With these conditions given as hypothesis, it wasn't too difficult to come up with a workable solution, to finalize a technique still employed in the 1980s. It was conceived by the brain trust in one Sunday afternoon session. Three men would be involved.

Simply run a hose from the faucet to a 20- or 25-gallon tub placed in the center of the tennis court surface. One skilled worker both controls the hose and dumps substantial quantities of calcium chloride from 25- or 100-pound bags into the water in the tub. A second skilled technician, using a long stick of wood, stirs the ingredients to uniform solution, while the third individual does the legwork. He scoops the solution from the tub and slings it from his pail as evenly as possible over the surface. One who does this for a decade is bound to get proficient at it.

Another technique, and one that is equally effective, is merely that of hosing the chloride after it has been broadcast in flake form over the surface. While this method can be employed at any time of day, the inadequacy of the water supply discourages such procedure. The limitation in available volume prompted advisory board member Lou Pingalore to suggest the fire department as a possible water source. Arrangements were subsequently and frequently made with the cooperative department, whose trucks have come to the rescue many times during a couple of decades now, spraying hundreds of gallons of water over the calcium applied just prior to their arrival. Former Deputy Fire Chief Calvin Cobb, a notable local tennis enthusiast, has been extremely helpful in this effort.

Obviously, such accommodation between the Fire and Recreation departments, though admirable and profoundly appreciated, cannot be a permanent solution in the long run. The fire trucks are not always available and their very important commitments are greatest at precisely the time when tennis courts and other fields are the driest—therefore, the inevitable reliance upon the extraordinary innovation of the brain trust, pail slinging, which is not so farfetched and impractical as one might suspect. Grant that it's a weird-looking process, an anachronism in this day and age perhaps, but really not. (After all, in reverse situations bath towels are frequently used to mop up water on fast-drying courts after downpours at sophisticated places.) Also, broadcasting the calcium solution in this manner by volunteer workers requires less time than one might think. With dedicated, unskeptical, uncritical enthusiasts like George Ulrich, Dick Marien, and Dr. Fred Eadie on hand, one tennis court can be treated with this clay-preserving chloride in about thirty minutes—four courts in the short space of two hours. The number of treatments per season depends on weather patterns, of course, but under the worst conditions no more than four or five applications are required. If periodic rains occur at optimum intervals it is unnecessary to introduce calcium in substantial quantities. Ideal timing of precipitation in desired amounts, however, has not been the format at Mohegan Park in over three decades of existence of the tennis courts, the clay surface of which long since would have been blown by the winds into adjacent woods and washed down the drains by cloudbursts had not the chloride been used consistently.

But even though the rains are conveniently spaced, it is important that some calcium chloride is applied to the surface, for more than preservation of the surface and eradication of dust and dried-out clay particles are involved. Anyone who has worked with this calcium salt knows how sticky the flakes become when they begin to absorb moisture. It is understandable, therefore, that the substance acts as an important binding agent as well, adding significantly to firmness and durability. And it also makes for excellent preparation of the surface for any kind of granular top dressing, aiding considerably in preventing Redkote, for example, from blowing away during gusty winds. In addition, when calcium chloride is integrated into the clay the top dressing retains a more uniform color and results in a better-looking tennis court. When applied in solution, its many advantages, when used sensibly, seem to be augmented—at least at Mohegan Park.

Despite the many advantages of broadcasting calcium after it is dissolved in water, this system used at the municipal courts would seldom be employed if an adequate water supply was available, for hosing the chloride thoroughly after it has been spread over the surface is equally effective. It's a good thing the brain trust came up with a workable system because it is essential that the playing area be as firm as possible. Municipal tennis courts take an awful pounding; the surface needs to be tough and capable of withstanding all kinds of traffic. Ideally, public clay facilities should be designed not only to take punishment from tennis neophytes of all ages but also to provide reasonable playability for advanced players. Beginners incline to beat up the courts to a far greater extent than the veterans.

Novices for the most part play in the middle of the court and few wear acceptable tennis shoes, which are comparatively expensive. The all-purpose shoes with accentuated corrugated soles, advertised and sold in most stores as footwear that serves for running, jogging, basketball, volleyball, tennis, hiking, and what have you, are pretty rough on clay courts. But it's too much to expect the beginner, particularly the youngsters, to purchase standard clay-court tennis sneakers for play on public courts. They buy the all-purpose shoes in good faith and believe them to be satisfactory for tennis, irrespective of the type of surface.

All this is not to say that experienced players with proper equipment do not on occasion punish the courts excessively, for there are the serve and volley specialists who raise havoc around the service-line area, obliterating the painted lines. And a high-level doubles match will often administer a severe beating to any surface other than bituminous or concrete. In addition, there are some perennials who are simply heavy-footed and who, like Peter Pappas, will dig up a clay court regardless of the footwear. The observation, sometimes advanced by players noting the beat-up condition of one of the courts, that "Peter has been here" is not always without basis in fact.

In view of the broad and all-inclusive types of play on public courts, it is clearly important if a clay surface is involved that it be as durable as possible—hence the premium placed on the introduction of calcium chloride and in this case on the pail-slinging procedure as well. One is inclined to believe that a better system could be devised for this accomplishment. No doubt scientists or engineers, if so disposed, could design equipment or machinery that would make slinging the solution out of the tub with a pail obsolete. But such has been the ultimate technique that the brain trust could devise.

The same commentary could be made, no doubt, in respect to the tennis court lines of linseed oil and traffic paint that have been laid down by hand now for well over two decades with ordinary two-inch paint brushes. Other techniques have been tried such as endeavoring the job with line-painting equipment and using rollers instead of brushes, but all have been unsatisfactory. And failure to come up with a better system has discouraged many potential volunteers from participation. Recreation Department personnel, provisions for whom have become greater over the years, are frequently turned off also. Some habitually call in "sick" on the days line painting is scheduled.

One may also inquire as to why tapes, which today are far superior to those used at the Home-Ec courts in the mid-1930s, are not used at the municipal courts instead of painted lines. It's primarily because tapes would not work out very well. They are usually secured with aluminum nails staggered from side to side at close intervals. A good-sized pailful of these nails, approximately 2,000, is required for one court. And these nails can't be driven through stones no matter the weight of the hammer, the brain trust having failed herein in its one and only experience with tapes. For this simple reason, along with a few others to be mentioned subsequently, the commitment has been to linseed oil and traffic paint.

Perhaps it is not inappropriate here to spell out in some detail what precisely is involved in laying down these lines in the spring. Some special qualifications exist in this situation as follows: first, the system fails if it cannot be done with reasonable dispatch; second, it also fails if the expense is too great. Also, the lines must be durable, capable of remaining secure from day to day so that the job does not require incessant redoing as in the case of dry or wet lime. For the most part, the painted lines satisfy the prerequisites.

Obviously, the surface must first have been cleaned and rolled, stones removed, and imperfections repaired. Removal of the previous year's lines is part of the cleaning process, for painted lines will not survive the winter. They are heaved by frost, which severs the bond from the base, reacting just as the stones, which are forced upwards and become exposed.

The next task is that of measuring out the court accurately, establishing extremities and intersections. It's superfluous to discuss the steps involved here, for the procedure to be followed is available in official publications of the United States Lawn Tennis Association or in most any library. Suffice it to say that with a couple of capable teenagers to hold the end of the steel measuring tape and fetch 10- or 12-inch spikes, the job takes at most twenty minutes—

somewhat less the two-hundredth time around. Rugged carpenter's string is then drawn from spike to spike at the corners as well as other intersections, and the court, 78 by 36 feet, is thus laid out completely, including service courts and doubles alleys, with the rugged twine. It is important that the string be drawn very taut and wound securely around the spikes before they are driven flush with the surface. By this time no more than another ten minutes has transpired. The preliminary work has now been completed and everything is set for the linseed oil and traffic paint, one court alone requiring a 480-foot application of each with 2-inch brushes.

Offhand this task may appear to be an astronomical backbreaker. But, though tough on the back, it is not astronomical. Depending on the condition of the surface (when too dry or porous it takes a little longer), the job is finished anywhere between thirty and forty minutes. At least three capable workers are needed if completion is to fall within this time frame. With their ordinary paint brushes two workmen apply a two-inch-wide layer of linseed, using the carpenter's string as a guide. They work together on one line at a time, always applying to the inside and taking care that the oil just reaches the taut guideline. If they get a little sloppy on the interior side it doesn't matter too much, for only the outside of the line is critical in tennis. The third worker puts down the traffic paint almost immediately following, not too soon, not too late. Application is facilitated when the timing is right, when the linseed has partially but not completely penetrated. And, as in the case of the linseed oil, care must be taken to paint up to, but not over, the guideline.

One may question the assertion that a complete set of lines can be laid down by three or four workers in thirty or forty minutes. After all, there are two applications, one of linseed, one of paint, amounting to 960 linear feet per court. But the facts are accurately stated. In a work session, for example, several years ago, a few members of the volunteer corps both measured and lined all four courts on one Saturday afternoon. Experienced and dedicated personnel, of course, workers such as Danny Bargnesi, were on the firing line—all of whom by then having know-how and expertise. The elapsed time involved is in direct proportion to the degree and attainment of a special dexterity with the brushes. It's different from painting a house. One shouldn't stand in the same place maneuvering the paint brush over that segment of line. One or two swipes a couple of feet in length is enough, then dip into the container and move on. This technique reduces the time span, is easier on the back, and makes for a better job. There's need only to apply the linseed; it will penetrate and solidify by itself. And too much brushing in the same area is apt to leave an undesirable groove.

No more than an hour and a quarter transpires from the first step in the measuring process to the last stroke of the traffic-paint brush. The lines will dry sufficiently for play in twenty-four to forty-eight hours, depending on weather conditions, and with periodic repair and "touching up" will last for the entire season. More of this later on.

Perhaps it should be mentioned here that it's unnecessary to apply traffic paint immediately following the linseed oil. There are two ways of doing it, one as just spelled out in brief outline. The other is simply that of laying down the linseed alone, letting it dry and solidify, and returning to the court after three or four days with paint and brushes for the white lines. This system works out very well and has some advantages. But it has proven too time consuming for the volunteer task force at the municipal multicourt complex. Some steps have to be repeated such as, for example, restretching the guidelines. For one who is fortunate enough to own a private court, however, this procedure is recommended. The result is somewhat better, the lines look great, and for a longer period of time before any repainting or "touching up" is required.

So much for some of the techniques entailed in putting down painted lines as well as one important advantage in the system, namely, the minimal time required to do the job. However, there are significant other attributes, the cost of the essential materials being especially pertinent. One gallon of linseed oil is more than sufficient for a single tennis court, and a gallon of traffic paint is adequate for two courts. All this amounted to less than ten dollars per court for an entire season in the 1950s and 1960s. And though somewhat higher now in the 1980s, expenditures on this score are much less per annum than the cost and installation of tapes or other alternatives, which have also increased in price.

Contrary to what one might suspect, the painted lines are surprisingly tough and durable, and will remain firm under most of the pressure from the soles of reasonably acceptable tennis shoes. And they are virtually impervious to any type of rain or storm. Moreover, there's no protrusion of the lines above the level of the court, and thus they do not cause bad bounces—as do most tapes when the tennis ball hits the edges. The lines, far from being disturbed by hand or power roller, are improved by the use of such equipment integrating them with the surrounding surface. This highly favorable property, along with the fact that painted lines are unsurpassed in appearance when satisfactorily maintained, represents one of their indisputable assets.

On the minus side, however, it must be stated that periodic repainting is necessary. They will discolor somewhat after heavy rains and after calcium chloride is applied to the courts—in whatever manner. But only the traffic paint is required this time around. Moreover, it is thinned with gasoline, flows on smoothly, and dries in fifteen minutes. It is easy, therefore, to "put down new lines" during a tournament or just before the finals. This is not to say that complete repainting is very often in order. Usually only the lines that take incessant beating, base lines and service lines particularly, need continual periodic attention. Sometimes more than just traffic paint is required when the linseed oil base itself becomes severely damaged. Imperfections, occasionally total eradication in places, caused by the heavy-footed may be such as to call for new clay in those areas and consequently another linseed base. Although far from a major operation and not often necessary, this work clearly represents a limitation in the system.

There's still more to be said on the negative side, the sum total of which is probably sufficient to explain why painted lines have been shortlived elsewhere. They should not be applied to surfaces that are too granular or porous and would be inappropriate for Har-Tru or En-Tous-Cas courts or anything comparable. Nor should lines of linseed oil and traffic paint be laid down too early in the spring because any subsequent severe frost will throw them off, breaking the bond with the clay base and necessitating another time around. This qualification is irrevocably inculcated in the minds of the brain trust, the boys having had to do the job all over again on more than one occasion.

When the system was first adopted the volunteers elected to put down the lines one year on court number "one" in late March. It was an early spring and the surface was in acceptable condition, having been prepared and rolled. The linseed-oil-and-traffic-paint procedure worked smoothly enough and the brain trust, looking forward to a sooner than usual start of the tennis season, was pleased with the result. But admiration of their work proved to be woefully transient. The lines had scarcely dried when the weather took an unfortunate turn. The few days of winter temperatures that followed introduced a couple of inches of frost in the ground and the lines, which once looked so good, became severed from the base. They would peel off in three- or four-foot lengths. This unhappy development had the effect of severing faith in the system itself as well. Even the most dedicated of the brain trust were turned off and frankly asked to be counted out if any subsequent attempt to apply linseed oil and traffic paint was made. It proved to be a difficult year for this advisory board member who committed himself to continuation of the line-painting procedure later on when the weather warmed up—and with little or no assistance. It was the first and last time this task was endeavored in the month of March.

Satisfactory maintenance of the municipal tennis courts requires that consistent attention is paid both to timely introduction of calcium chloride and care of the painted lines. If department personnel, together with volunteer assistance from brain trust enthusiasts, keep abreast of these two major tasks, the city of Norwich can be assured of good-looking, remarkably durable facilities that afford excellent playability across the board. But there's another facet to maintenance outside of the routine brushing and rolling of the courts that is also an important part of the upkeep. Reference is made to illicit play when the tennis complex is closed and locked during and immediately after rains, when the courts are destined to suffer extensive damage. They are most vulnerable when the sun comes out for the first time after a few days of continual rain and impatient players are anxious to get going forthwith. The fact that the complex is locked represents no deterrent, for many are those who will negotiate the enclosure, going over, under, or through the fences onto the soft and wet surface. Nor do "Courts Closed" placards hung on the gates have much of an impact.

If a tennis game is going on inside the locked premises the manner of entrance is conclusive, and one is frequently amazed when those who climbed or tunneled their way in are identified. Never is one found digging up a soft surface who has ever assisted in repair work, however. Sometimes an incredible story unfolds. Once a former tennis enthusiast, having given up the game ten years previously, decided for unknown reasons that it was high time he started playing again. Apparently his decision to begin on a certain day was irrevocable, for he was observed stroking tennis balls inside the closed courts in the rain. One supposes that his resolution was so momentous that he couldn't possibly wait another day for clearing skies.

Less interesting is the fence-climbing player who starts his game on a selected court and abandons it after the surface is dug up to the point that the tennis ball bounces erratically. He then moves on to the next court, leaving it in shambles before trying a third and possibly a fourth. This demolition process requires only about thirty minutes—unless someone with authority spots the intruder in the interim. Generally speaking, trespassers invariably wear the roughest-soled track shoes available, also.

The Home-Ec courts, where there is no surveillance whatsoever except for an occasional check, are particularly vulnerable on this score. And it is comparatively easy to climb the chain-link fence. Moreover, youngsters are attracted to the large puddles created by heavy downpours. They like to play in the water and some really enjoy pushing the hand roller through the shallow pools. This exercise, while exciting for the kids, does not exactly simplify the maintenance task.

The Recreation Department at long last is now able to provide for surveillance at the municipal courts during and immediately after rainy weather and therefore this problem is largely alleviated at the park. But the tennis court supervisor has to be on the lookout constantly, nonetheless. Sometimes the place will be invaded before he arrives—by ambitious early birds who have completed the wrecking job prior to 8:00 A.M. Occasionally, one of the five gates will have been inadvertently left unlocked, giving the enthusiasts easy and purportedly legitimate access to the courts, regardless of the degree of precipitation.

Throughout his many years of observation, this advisory board member is convinced that the frequent damage to unplayable tennis courts seldom represents deliberate vandalism, however. Rather it's primarily the story of the impatient player who reacts to the clear weather sooner than does the clay surface. This is not to say that the tennis complex has always been immune from outright vandalism. Once a low-bed, the conveyance used to transport bulldozers, was unbraked in the parking lot and rolled down over the bank through the fence onto court number "four" (now number "six"). And one of the tennis nets was ruined one time by the imaginative technique of lighting a fire to it. "Like burning the flag," remarked Judge Brown. But the unsought activity most often occurs outside the courts proper, the portable bleachers taking an incessant beating. They are forever tipped over, sometimes wrecked, and occasionally one will be found removed from its habitat in the middle of Mohegan Road.

However, when compared to some other areas, both here and elsewhere, deliberate acts of vandalism have not been of the crisis variety at Recreation Field, nor has the damage inflicted on the unplayable tennis court surfaces by the adventurers who penetrate the fences. It is true that on occasion an inordinate amount of work and effort is required to rejuvenate the courts and one is often inclined to remonstrate and blast the intruders in no uncertain terms—particularly when the painted lines are severely damaged, which will happen when the surface is wet and soft. But one should not overreact in this situation. Far better to adopt a low-key tone, difficult though it may be, and enumerate the reasons why digging up a tennis court makes little sense. It is helpful to point out that considerable additional work is involved—and with reserved objective intonation. And it is important to remember that the most vehement reprimand does not assist the repair operation, which has to be done in any event. Once in a while this approach pays off immediately when the perpetrators offer to help rectify the damage.

There have been some exceptions to the general rule that indicates the folly of overreacting to unpleasant developments. While rolling the courts one Saturday afternoon in early spring this advisory board member noticed two individuals emerge from an automobile, which had been driven into the parking lot, and approach the tennis courts with rackets and balls preparatory for play. The facilities were a far cry from being ready, however—no nets were up, no lines were down, and the courts were soggy. Since this was assumed to be obvious to anyone, the rolling procedure continued without interruption. But when the two individuals, one male, one female, in their late teens or early twenties, walked onto one of the courts and began to stroke some tennis balls, the board member stopped the Gravely tractor, which was pulling the roller, to inform the pair that the courts were not yet open. (Apparently there are some tennis buffs for whom neither lines nor nets are necessary.) The male participant acted and responded as though he personally owned the courts, and while such an attitude was not objectionable and in fact almost commonplace and even appreciated, since the facilities are public, he was politely informed that it would be at least a week before opening day. Care was taken to speak with low-key, reserved intonation as usual. But when the board member was berated and asked why he didn't somehow relate this information "when you saw me get out of the automobile," this became one of the occasions that turned out to be an exception to the general rule that upholds equanimity and composure.

Enough, perhaps, has been said about the unfortunate aspects of extracurricular activity to indicate that there are other facets to maintenance than upkeep of the painted lines and the periodic introduction of calcium chloride. And then, too, there's always the stone-removal exercise in the spring. The annual April workouts of throwing out those which have been heaved through the surface were once thought to be transitory, that eventually there'd be virtually none in evidence after the winter months. Such has not been the case, however, for though progressively fewer, the stones still come up every year. One speculator has advanced the theory that they constantly arrive from China, traveling 8,000 miles through the core of the earth, emerging each spring on the municipal courts for him to pick up and carry away. Despite the eloquence and persuasiveness of this dissertation, the story is rather that the stones arrived on the site across the surface of the earth rather than through it, and did not come from China. Half came from city travel banks via Selectman Dorsey's trucks, and the other half from Sterling Mott's farm.

Whatever the case, those who comprised that loose organization of volunteers with rotating membership, referred to as the brain trust, came gradually to a more comfortable repose in Sunday afternoon executive sessions. They were getting used to the annual tasks of throwing out the stones and subsequent line painting. And most of the one-time apparently insurmountable obstacles that were high on the agenda in previous sessions had been resolved. Though full of those confounded stones, the clay, once thought to be unattainable, now covered the entire area in reasonable depth. And the difficulties relating to the limitations in water pressure and volume had been alleviated by applying calcium chloride in solution. Moreover, the painted white lines stood out strikingly against the background of Redkote top dressing, and surprisingly the whole complex looked very good.

Not only did the place look good, but also it began to dawn on the boys that the tennis courts were now a first-class public facility. The brain trust members also came to realize that the integration of bank gravel and clay made for a toughness of surface ideal for a municipal complex. Youngsters could race over the courts all day, beginners wearing those rough-soled all-purpose shoes could punish the courts incessantly, and later the same day the facilities were very satisfactory for advanced players of any level. A quick brushing of the surface with a six-foot drag brush and a fast sweeping of the white lines was enough. The volunteers have been happy about this interesting accidental development, and very appropriately so. That the courts have turned out to be a true public facility that can be administered in the direction of all-inclusive use is very important to the Recreation Advisory Board and the city council in Norwich. We have been glad that the tennis complex has served such a broad range of area residents without any fee or hourly charge.

If the preponderance of gravel in the actual playing surface has worked out as an asset, and the volunteers believe it has, perhaps the stones in the clay from Sterling Mott's farm may be advantageous, also. At least, some of the boys have so theorized. While such an assumption cannot be substantiated and is probably false, distribution of the clay by hand seems to have been preferable, nonetheless. When the chunks of clay are so distributed, the material is deposited over the base very much in the form of its birthplace in the bank. Any screening process that could get rid of the stones might have had the effect of breaking down the original cohesiveness and therefore detracting from firmness and solidity. While this may well be rationalization after the fact, it has made for a sense of satisfaction for the laborer-scientists, even though the procedure was born of necessity and not deliberately planned.

Whether all this is true or not, we have had to grapple with the stones at Mohegan Park, for better or worse. A few will work their way up over the general level of the surface in the course of the summer and become exposed after heavy rains. And for some, the sight of a stone is a telltale disclosure, suggesting lack of sophistication and indicative of poor construction—a botch job. But there's nothing wrong with stones in the surface, providing they don't protrude above it. Grant that some will work their way to the top during the course of summer play to the point they have to be removed, leaving holes of various sizes. However, these can easily be filled with clay in nothing flat if skilled members of the brain trust like Joe Lonardelli and Cal Cobb are around. There are various ways of doing this; the one used most effectively has been with the hand trowel after softening new clay with calcium chloride in solution. Troublesome stones observed just prior to tournament, when there's insufficient time for the removal-and-hole-filling operation, can be driven back out of sight with a sledgehammer, still another ingenious technique conceived by the scientists. They know from experience that said stones will show up another time when they can be removed.

13

Clinics, Tournaments, and the Return to NFA

Having come up with a good-looking and acceptable complex at long last, and having observed its serviceability for players across the board, brain trust members next turned to the more enjoyable matters of programming and planning activities. There were two major areas for consideration. First and foremost was the proposition of stimulating interest in the game as a recreational exercise for the general public; second, there was the formalized tournament play. In planning introduction of the game and instruction for the people, it was decided to start with a series of free Monday night clinics. The program turned out to be tremendously popular and was continued for a few years until the Recreation budget was sufficient to provide for daily clinics run by the department during summer months.

The Monday night sessions were run by well-known Miss Dorothy O'Neil (subsequently ranked in the top ten in New England), Stanley Bierylo, and Dick Korenkiewicz, along with this advisory board member. The clinics were something to behold. Attendance usually exceeded 100 individuals—predominantly youngsters, some of whom would arrive with badminton rackets, squash rackets, and Ping-Pong paddles. A few would simply race over the premises, one end to the other at breakneck speed. Instruction proceeded, but not without difficulty. When asked about the worth and advisability of continuation of the program, Henri Salaum (New England's number-one-ranking player for many years, who once observed the show) responded definitely in the affirmative. "If nothing else, you've succeeded in getting them on a tennis court." For the vast majority, nonetheless, there was something accomplished in the way of sound instruction—particularly for the adults, many of whom became real enthusiasts. How much the clinics had to do with all this cannot be known exactly, but a couple of basic facts were obvious, namely that the program never could have taken place without existence of the facilities, which at the least enabled instructors to teach the group how to keep score.

As to tournament play and other formalized competition, the decision to move in this direction also was made without dissenting votes. Organization of the Norwich Tennis Association and membership in the United States Lawn Tennis Association having been established in 1956, it was easy to gain legitimate sanction for regional championships and the first eastern Connecticut event in Norwich occurred that year. The moguls of the brain trust were careful not to go overboard in this direction, however. For it was important to bear in mind that the makeshift courts, no matter the virtual absence of cost to the taxpayers, were public facilities and not built primarily as a site for sanctioned tournaments. But there's another and important side to this, because the townspeople would be in many ways the beneficiaries of these events. Perhaps the most significant here is the fact that the city continues to be the recipient of facilities in reasonably good condition. Having committed themselves, it has been incumbent upon the committee members to "snap to," introduce calcium chloride where necessary, repaint the lines, apply top dressing, and come up with courts acceptable for tournament play. Almost certainly, were it not for these annual sanctioned tournaments, the whole tennis complex might well have been shortlived. There's a deadline to meet, extra effort is entailed, and if the courts are adequate for the finest players in New England they would be equally satisfactory for local people.

There are other advantages that strengthen the case for the tournaments. For example, the game is really introduced to the community, the potentialities of the sport demonstrated, and general interest is stimulated. Conversely, the community is introduced to the region in proportion to the extent of the areas from which participants come. Tournaments help put the city "on the map." And those who run them assist both the sectional and national associations in their programs as well.

Therefore, in addition to the annual city tournaments for juniors and adults, it was decided to continue on with the Eastern Connecticut Championships. In fact, an additional sanctioned event, the Connecticut State Senior Championships (participants age forty-five and over) were held beginning in 1957 and for a few years thereafter—when the load got to be a little too much. This was a very special and significant period in the history of tennis in New England and not peculiar to Norwich, Connecticut. Comparable efforts were then in process in some other places, most of whose courts were enclosed by more sophisticated and aesthetic fences. But embarrassment or sensitivity in respect to our improvised structure, attached to posts from the junk yards, never occurred to anyone. It served the basic purpose about as well as any fence elsewhere—although a barrier somewhat easier for players the caliber of Jules Cohen to bounce an overhead smash outside the premises in places where the wiring sagged between the uprights.

Lack of artistic beauty of the enclosure was compensated for by the appearance of the courts, which generally were in good shape for the tournaments. And while they were not as good as they looked, and better the more distant the viewer, the painted white lines stood out strikingly and enhanced the aesthetic aspect of the complex. Any keen observer, however, could easily come up with a fairly accurate history of the place, readily noting that it was the result of a succession of piecemeal, fragmented, expedient operations by volunteers. But all this was both understandable and appropriate. The relative status of tennis at the time was just about in accordance with the manner in which the courts were constructed. Everything was commensurate. The game was such a poor relation in municipal recreation that use of the best tools and equipment could not be justified. Tennis was all right if facilities were built gratuitously by hand and played after hours or on holidays. Any effort to obtain adequate governmental appropriations for courts would be regarded as almost sacrilegious. If legislators ever sponsored such allocations they wouldn't be long for the council chamber.

It would be some time before significant appropriations would be adopted by the Norwich municipality in the area of recreation generally—tennis requiring a longer waiting period. As in the case of virtually all actions by government it would be necessary to wait for the right time, to play the situation "by ear." The timing would be in accordance with both a recognized need and concomitant acceptance by the citizens. The psychological perspective of the people and their representatives must be on a common wave length for such innovations to come to pass. And in Norwich over two decades would transpire from the time the first net went up in 1950 before any major appropriation for tennis would be adopted.

From the time of the start of the first sanctioned tournament in 1956, however, there were some surprising and encouraging developments that stimulated the volunteer workers. Aside from the growing interest in the game and increased use of the courts, there were occasional accolades from tournament players who were impressed with their playability. Well-known veterans of the tennis circuit like Paul Jenney of Feeding Hills, Massachusetts, and Walter Blauvelt of Middleton, Massachusetts, were strongly affirmative in their commendations. Blauvelt once remarked, after playing a total of ninety-five games one day on court number "one," that he did not receive one bad bounce in all that time.

But the communication that was most treasured was a letter from Irving Levine, then of Fall River, Massachusetts. The fabulous Mr. Levine, one of the steadiest players ever, was on an advisory committee in that city formed for the purpose of making recommendations to municipal officials in respect to contemplated tennis courts. His note indicated that of all the courts he had played on, he preferred those at Norwich, Connecticut, and was interested in the exact formula and specifications so that he could recommend same to the government in his home town. Any reader who has stuck with this story thus far can appreciate the virtual impossibility of spelling out a precise formula on paper. Each of the four tennis courts not only had a unique history but also a special base—three feet of Norwich bank gravel under number "one" phased out to a few inches under court number "two," to plain terrain for "three" and "four."

Whatever the prerequisites of each, they were equally satisfactory for Irving throughout the many long matches he played here—although none quite so extended as the five-and-a-half-hour, three-set match he once played in the Midwest against George Ball.

Although the few accolades received came mostly from the out-of-town tournament players and generally not from local people, the effort of the volunteers was apparently not lost on officials at the Norwich Free Academy. While the West Side Tennis Court on Forest Street was maintained for some time by Ted Montgomery, the so-called Home-Ec courts next to Judge Brown's backyard on Broadway had deteriorated over the years. They were a far cry from what they were in 1939 and 1940 when George Silverman won an early Norwich tournament there. George, who defeated Ogden Sawyer from Providence, Rhode Island, in the finals, always enjoyed the courts, but only after appropriate rains. However, by this time more than the introduction of periodic moisture would be required to return the surface to the condition it was in in the late 1930s. Many changes had taken place in the two decades since 1936. The hemlock trees, once neatly spaced, had grown about thirty feet as had other trees bordering on the fences. Cleaning up of leaves and debris would therefore be in order almost daily, particularly in the fall. The academy was still using the courts in its physical education program after engaging landscaper Hildebrand to condition the courts in the spring. But this was a one-shot operation on a complex requiring day-to-day attention. Understandably, the courts were a sorry sight during summer and fall months. Moreover, lack of consistent maintenance and play allowed moss to grow over much of the area. In addition, the clay laid down from the cement mixer in 1936 had lost much of its plasticlike texture, and additional material had been blown away over the years from winds in dry weather.

The decline and degeneration of the Home-Ec complex was not lost upon Principal George Shattuck and Buildings and Grounds Superintendent Theodore Kennedy. It was also apparent that all this was taking place at a time when interest and participation in tennis was on the increase. Since joint use of the municipal facilities at the park by NFA and the general public had been in vogue since 1951 and quite satisfactorily, it was logical to extend the arrangement to the Home-Ec courts. This advisory board member was approached accordingly and enthusiastically agreed to the proposition. The contemplated plan would be advantageous to all concerned. The Norwich Free Academy could forget about maintenance and still have courts available for gymnasium classes. As in the case at Recreation Field, the place would be reserved for any school program during the academic year but available to the public at all other times. NFA officials also agreed to participate in the cost of materials needed for maintenance purposes. From the standpoint of the municipality the new setup would be equally advantageous: two additional clay courts for general use, a 50 percent increase in facilities by virtue of a simple arrangement.

On the whole, the return to the Home-Ec after a twenty-year absence worked out very well and many are those who have spent enjoyable hours there. NFA students, meanwhile, though obviously limited in playing time because of the size of gym classes, were nonetheless introduced to the game as part of their education and in the process at least learned what an acceptable tennis court looks like. The cooperation of the NFA officials, who have been pleased with the results, has been superb. Comments such as one by Principal Shattuck soon after the plan was initiated to the effect that the courts looked better than at any time in ten years served only to improve relationships.

The volunteers of the brain trust enjoyed their new assignment, and they tackled the spring conditioning work with enthusiasm. Moreover, the men looked forward to the day when the nets went up, and play rather than work would be first on the agenda. In the early years of the NFA/advisory-board-member agreement, municipal maintenance personnel were unavailable, and it was necessary to rely completely on whatever manpower could be mustered. Seldom was there extensive planning established at a meeting of the executive board. Rather, the procedure was simply that of starting the job as early as possible on a spring evening and continuing on alone until a potential worker might show up. Those who did not have inescapable commitments elsewhere would be latched on to instantaneously. Two such individuals were Danny Bargnesi and Ken Church, to whom Norwich tennis players were then indebted. It is quite understandable that the conditioning process had to proceed in this unscientific manner. The limited maintenance staff was very much overextended then. Conditioning of all the recreational places, baseball and softball fields, playground and play areas descended on the department all at once every spring. Head maintenance man, Joe Boucher, consistently worked seven days a week. Now, in the 1980s, with more resources and a more realistic operating budget, this difficult situation has been somewhat, but by no means completely, alleviated.

A substantially different type of conditioning task presented itself at the Home-Ec. It was an easier one for the volunteers in that there were no stones to pick up and carry away. Also, it was helpful to to have an adequate water supply available; a city water faucet at the rear of the adjacent building provided a source with excellent pressure. It was therefore seldom necessary to apply calcium chloride in solution, since it could be broadcast in flake form and quickly dissolved by water from a hose. Introduction of calcium chloride has been an absolute necessity over the past two decades. For, as indicated earlier, the clay by then had lost its cohesiveness and badly needed this indispensable binder. At least eight or nine hundred pounds are needed for each court annually, an amount not always available and thus the optimum volume sometimes is not applied. It is advisable to spray the chloride thoroughly, but if the timing is right there may not be need for any hosing whatsoever. This would be the case when the calcium is spread just before the right kind of rain. All the prerequisites must be satisfied in order to accomplish this time-saving result—materials, equipment, manpower ready at the site, which has occurred infrequently in the history of Home-Ec maintenance. Once, when an appropriate rain appeared imminent, this advisory board member endeavored the operation alone. Two trips were made to Cash Home Center to obtain 1,000 pounds of calcium chloride, the 100-pound bags transported unsecured on the fenders of a Dodge Coronet. The bags were spotted and emptied on the courts and the flakes hurriedly broadcast over the surface in the nick of time. The rain clouds opened up on schedule but not for long, and an unanticipated clearing trend was observable as the sun's rays began to penetrate the overcast. Since the precipitation was far from adequate, the hose was connected quickly and the watering process initiated even before the rains ceased. At this point in time, Dr. Vincent Varone, tennis player and department head at NFA, arrived upon the scene, observing the municipal advisory official watering the facilities in the rain! The faculty member thought for sure that Home-Ec maintenance had scored the ultimate and final victory.

Whatever the case, it was the first and last time that both major sources of water, rain and hose, were used simultaneously for the purpose of introducing calcium chloride into the surface of the complex. In the last analysis, though, there is only one ultimate source, namely that from the skies. But the one via the circuitous route from the heavens to the reservoir, then through the trunk lines to the faucet is obviously preferable in this procedure. The faucet lends itself to deliberate control by man; thus timing and planning can be arbitrary, the chloride on the courts dissolved by the hose at will. There are, however, exceptions and qualifications to the assertion. The day before the start of one sanctioned tournament, for example, the busy volunteer task force was scheduled to apply some calcium to the surface of the Home-Ec that afternoon. Planning and timing were both perfect—manpower, materials, and hose arriving on the site as contemplated. The hose was connected and everything was "Go," but when the faucet was turned to the "on" position no water from the outlet was forthcoming. Extensive renovation, it turned out, was then under way in the interior of the Home-Ec Building, most of the plumbing having been ripped out in the process. There were no complimentary letters from tournament players as to the condition of those two courts that year.

This one-time failure of the water supply did not negate the comparative plus for the complex vis-à-vis the municipal courts from the standpoint of maintenance. The piping was rerouted in due course and adequate water available again, which along with the absence of stones made life easier for the volunteer court-conditioners in the spring. Throughout the average six- to seven-month annual season, however, it has been indelibly impressed upon those who have worked and played there that maintenance of the Home-Ec courts would be more difficult in the long run. Instead of the once yearly stone-removal operation at the city courts in the park, brushing off of debris from overhanging hemlocks and elms would be required daily. In late summer there's an additional item to be removed, namely black walnuts almost the size of tennis balls, which descend upon the premises from a walnut tree next to the fence on the east. The impact of the walnuts landing on workers or players from the gigantic branches above is greater than that of a Wilson or Dunlop.

In addition, these rare courts laid down from cement mixer in the mid-1930s have peculiar characteristics—perhaps not unlike many other clay facilities that have had little attention over two decades. Owing to the preponderance of trees along the fences and associated lack of sun plus a poorly functioning drainage well, the courts dry very slowly after rains to the point when playable. On the other hand, when dried out thoroughly, the surface turns to clay dust, which blows away even from the slightest atmospheric turbulence. Generally, the prevailing westerly winds are in the direction of the late Judge Brown's imposing white house, hence the perpetual need for the indispensable calcium chloride. The chief justice was all smiles when he observed the chloride going down, whatever the manner. Once after an inquiry as to why so much was being used, and after being told it helped preserve the courts, the knowledgeable judge responded immediately, "It preserves the paint on my house as well."

The preponderance of the clay dust on the courts has complicated the linseed-oil-and-traffic-paint lining operation. The linseed oil will solidify the clay but not to the depth necessary for durability. Solution of this problem has not been easy, for it has been necessary to dig up the areas where the lines go down and trowel in new red clay. Obviously, this has been a formidable task, which has not been accomplished in one operation. Rather it's been an ongoing exercise for some time and, at the time of this writing, almost complete.

Judge Allyn Brown, who worked over the years in his backyard virtually alongside the volunteer corps, and who spent little time observing either the conditioning process or the subsequent tennis, was nonetheless highly interested in the line-painting procedure. He had too much to do in his backyard; his life was too well organized to waste very much time watching what was going on. Yet he was far more observant than one might suspect. The judge, for example, once told this advisory official that he could easily detect the level of play from the frequency and intensity of the sound of ball against racket. Only an occasional glance to identify the participants was necessary to learn the whole story.

But more than a glance was required for his appreciation of lines of traffic paint. "How can you paint over dirt?" he once asked. After being informed of both the function and prior application of linseed oil, the system made more sense to the judge. Yet he remained a little skeptical until he observed how the lines worked out in practice, the one phase of conditioning he took time out to watch. The chief justice was ultimately convinced, however, and frequently would come forth with favorable comments as to the durability and straightness of the lines.

Enough, perhaps, of the pluses and minuses, the assets and liabilities, of the Home-Ec arrangement has now been said to provide a reasonably accurate picture. But there's an important one on the plus side that, although perhaps implied, needs a positive, definitive line. Simply stated, involvement with the courts there enabled one to get to know and attain friendship with a great man. Perhaps because of his awareness of the work and effort expended, much of which on afternoons of the Sabbath, perhaps because of his interest in healthy games such as tennis, or whatever else, a note was received at the insurance office of this advisory board member, which read as follows: "The NFA courts may be opened for play after 1:00 P.M. on Sundays until further notice." Signed, Judge Brown.

On the whole, playability at the Home-Ec courts generally has been fairly good after the volunteers arrived upon the scene. They were very satisfactory if properly taken care of, especially on an overcast day. Shadows from the surrounding gigantic trees have made for some limitations quite apart from the perennial debris they have bestowed upon us. When the sun is shining in the direction of the Home-Ec area, there is never a time when both courts are free from shadows. This detracts from the visibility of the tennis ball and bothers players of any level, beginners or advanced. Shadows are all right if they extend uniformly and completely over an entire court, but such is never the case at the NFA complex. And there is nothing worse than a mottled background, which, at certain times during sunny days, is the inescapable situation there. One of the first lessons taught by any tennis teacher is the importance of watching the ball carefully and incessantly, which is difficult enough under ideal conditions let alone on facilities where the background is now dark, then light, then dark again. Particularly for beginners there's always the tendency to take the "eye off the ball" while making the actual stroke and look up too soon to see where it's going. Mottled shadows only compound the problem.

Although the Home-Ec courts were needed and used for the annual tournaments, players frequently objected to playing matches there for this reason. Nonetheless, the shadows always served a purpose even for the participants—the ones who lost, that is, 50 percent of them, have had the alibi of poor visibility. And while said visibility is obviously the same for both winner and loser, any experienced tournament chairman knows that many have more difficulties than others on this score. The experienced chairman also knows it's the losers who are affected the most. Yet some of the winners, if losers in the next round, will frequently refer to the same excuse.

The alibiers have a point, however, and poor visibility is bothersome and does affect some more than others. Vision is not a constant, and varies from individual to individual. Even all-around athlete Roger Marien and this advisory board member, who had a standing engagement in singles each weekday evening for nearly a decade, would play matches at the Home-Ec only on overcast or cloudy days. If it was clear with sun shining, the confrontation was always on the municipal courts at Mohegan Park. This format was not always adhered to, for athlete Roger was also involved in city league baseball throughout much of this period. Whatever the situation in the heavens, cloudy or otherwise, Rog Marien, an infielder par excellence, preferred the city courts on evenings he was scheduled for baseball. After two or three sets, he would cross Mohegan Road to the Recreation Building, quickly change into his baseball gear, and proceed to the adjacent ball field for a subsequent athletic endeavor. One is exceptionally gifted who is that versatile, and it is interesting that Roger, who is also a fine golfer, credited his tennis playing prior to city league games for higher batting averages during some of those years.

All of this added up to an interesting period in the late 1950s.

By then we had seven pretty good clay tennis courts: four municipal, the two at the Home-Ec, and the West Side Tennis Court off Forest Street. All the facilities were available to the people and were also acceptable for the running of tournaments. Moreover, the volunteer corps remained formidable and it wasn't difficult to recruit new members. Over that span, membership not only increased, but workers gained knowledgeability and expertise. No longer was spring conditioning regarded as a prohibitive chore. True, we had to throw out the stones and fill the holes at Recreation Field and introduce new clay at the Home-Ec, seven courts in all to roll, measure out, and line with oil and traffic paint. True also, a lot of work was entailed and speed in accomplishment more of the essence, but by then speed had been attained. While there had been a time when conditioning and line painting of just one court was considered a major conquest, this was no longer the case. By 1959 it was simply routine, even though there were a couple of times when yellow rather than white traffic paint was delivered by those dispatched to the hardware store!

In the meantime, the Department of Recreation was in the process of being established as a legitimate function of government and Phil Booker had been appointed as the first director on a year-round basis. He replaced the indefatigable Bill Kelly, who headed the department previously, operating full-time during summer months and part-time for the balance of the year. Bill's energy and dedication had much to do with the popularization of Recreation as well as subsequent increases in budget allocations. His accomplishments were the more remarkable in that all the while he was a full-time faculty member and coach at NFA.

As the budget increased so did the resources of the department, which at long last was able to assign personnel to assist in the maintenance of the courts. In fact, Phil Booker himself frequently would find the time to pitch in personally, particularly in the spring. Additional assistance during this period was forthcoming from the boys who comprised the Norwich Free Academy tennis squad. The theory was that the April workouts raking up and removing stones and debris and helping out in the linseed-oil-and-traffic-paint exercise was an important part of their indoctrination, and they would later appreciate the clay courts accordingly. Although none of the youngsters were products of the pick-and-shovel era, nor were the tennis coaches, they nonetheless helped out considerably and gained at least some background and knowledge of consequence. It was important to assign the right boy to the appropriate task if an acceptable result was to be achieved. Few, obviously and understandably, had extensive experience with an ordinary paint brush, but invariably there were some who had done some painting around the house at home, and who would be assigned to applying linseed oil. Others had no background with hammer and spikes, yet there were always one or two. And there were always a few capable kids who had no training or experience in anything comparable to the work involved. Verbal or philosophical assignments were for them. Clever ones emerged from the work sessions in good standing amongst their teammates without exercising anything but the vocal cords.

Because of their heavy academic commitments the tennis coaches, with but one or two exceptions, were usually absent during the spring conditioning process. They would assign boys to the work who "went out" for tennis, make note of their presence, and forthwith depart from the scene. Educational responsibilities come first, and apparently there's no way that picking up stones, cleaning up debris, or pushing a hand roller can be construed as education. One coach somewhere along the line stayed long enough one spring afternoon not only to observe the horrendous mess, but also to inquire when "these things" would be ready for play. It was interesting to note that when the nets eventually went up on "these things" the academic load was not so demanding.

It was infrequent that potential members of the first team were sent to the clay courts to assist in the conditioning procedure. They would be off practicing somewhere on hard courts, which are always playable except during or immediately after rains or when covered with snow. And when the lines were down and the nets up the first-stringers would return and take over the facilities. There have been at least a few occasions when some of those who decided they would go out for tennis and who were assigned to court conditioning quit the squad before playing any tennis whatsoever on the courts they helped prepare.

An unbelievably wide gap in respect to the level of capability at the game exists between the varsity players and the beginners. It's like comparing the neighborhood Sunday afternoon touch football quarterback to Dan Fouts of the San Diego Chargers or Joe Ferguson of the Buffalo Bills. Some of the boys, such as Dave Coletti of Norwich or Scott Slobin of Hartford, developed a high degree of skill very early in life. Coletti, for example, won the city of Norwich regular men's singles title at age thirteen, before he even entered high school.

None of this has been lost upon Norwich Free Academy's current tennis coach, Gil LaPointe, who simply does not have the time to introduce the game across the board. Gil, like any other coach, is under some pressure to attain a respectable winning percentage in interscholastic competition, which is the traditional criterion of a coach's effectiveness. Thus he understandably devotes his time and energy to improving the play of those who already have a tennis background, for there is generally no way that the game of a raw beginner can be developed to the point where he could gain a singles or doubles berth on the first team.

It is not the purpose here to treat this subject extensively except to point out that tennis, like golf, is probably a special case in high school, if not in college. There are no "walk-ons" who occasionally surprise the coaching staff, as in football. There are no major upsets animated by "getting up" for a match when there exists a significant difference in capability. The successful coaches in individual head-to-head competition are usually the ones who inherit or recruit talent, in the original development of which they rarely have much or any influence. The kids who have grown up in encouraging environments, frequently the beneficiaries of professional instruction, comprise the team.

One therefore is inclined to believe that interscholastic competition can be overemphasized—particularly in the boys' division to which most of the above is directed. This is not to say that the game should not be a part of the athletic curriculum in the schools, for tennis has a great deal going for it. Introduction to the so-called carry-over sports and their lifelong benefits and challenge is important. What is needed is a different approach in these areas—more emphasis on the introductory and instructional side, less exclusive use of the facilities by a comparative few. Interscholastic competition should be more than a vehicle to aggrandize further those who have attained significant capability, and should involve more players.

These observations point up two aspects of tennis in secondary schools. There is the interscholastic team activity, which has some unfortunate facets. (Spring conditioning of the Norwich courts by second-team kids is now not one of these—recreational maintenance personnel in recent years have been able to handle this work.) On the other hand, it is important to introduce the game for what it is primarily—namely, an excellent carry-over athletic activity. The scrimmage games such as football and basketball do not fall within this category. As in any sport, however, or for that matter in most any human endeavor, it's ridiculous to rule out or discount the competitive element. One doesn't play, work, or participate on this planet in a vacuum. And in the athletic arena tennis is perhaps one of the ultimate illustrations, for it's head-to-head competition of a high order. It is a game where victory and status are clearly defined and conclusive. Even golf is not so highly individualized, for one is playing the course to a great extent, rather than his opponent. It is easy to see, therefore, why beginners in tennis easily become discouraged and why some not only quit the squad but quit the game. The point, it is believed here, and one which is easier to write about than for a coach to achieve in actual practice, is simply that the introductory side should receive more attention in respect to carry-over sports, not that team competition should be eliminated.

14

A Parking Lot at Recreation Field

The volunteer corps did not belabor its collective acumen about the philosophical aspects of the game of tennis, however, for maintenance of all the clay courts remained number one on the agenda. And the time came, also, when upgrading and sprucing up of the grounds outside the courts proper became an important matter for consideration, particularly to the east where an area of about 50,000 square feet was earmarked for a parking lot. Although needed primarily for baseball games (the field is just across Mohegan Road), the place was so situated that it would provide parking for tennis and other activities as well. Until 1958 this area was both a mess and an eyesore.

Preoccupation with the courts per se was a major reason for this condition. The area had been used as a dumping place for excess material throughout construction of the courts, the city grader and dump trucks having left piles of various kinds strewn all over the premises. This advisory board member, then chairman, decided it was high time to eliminate the mess and come up with an acceptable parking facility. Consummation of the project took place the summer of that year, and in retrospect, while not an achievement of any great magnitude, it was at the very least a fairly important accomplishment. Too big a job to tackle with pick and shovel on weekends, the board member was committed to proceed through the governmental channels under the council-manager regime—although there would be one or two times when direct assault with the hand tools appeared the more expeditious route.

City Manager Jay Etlinger was persuaded to inspect the area along with the board chairman after office hours, and after a couple of visits he was convinced of the feasibility of the project, subsequently calling a meeting in his office with the director of Public Works, Harold Walz. The three of us agreed upon a general procedure. City equipment would be utilized to level and roughly grade the terrain to desired contour and pitch determined by administrative personnel, and the purchasing agent would obtain the best price for the right kind of gravel for a parking lot. Seymour Adelman of Fitchville was engaged accordingly. Public Works was too busy during the summer months to truck in the material, and, moreover, the gravel from the city banks supposedly was not of proper consistency for a parking lot, which required a mixture that would pack better than any composition available from local sources. The role of the Recreation Advisory Board chairman in the project was not yet concluded, however, for he became aware that Adelman would be arriving any day with the gravel from Fitchville, and before completed plans were forthcoming from Public Works establishing important provisions such as entrances and exits to the site.

The regular routine of driving by the roughly graded area several times daily was the only established maneuver. At least an advisory official would be on hand when the gravel came. The day when the first Adelman truck arrived was a busy one for the chairman, whose first assignment was the understandable one of directing the drivers to the best places to dump their loads. Next came a fast trip to the office of the city manager, who, of course, was tied up in high-level conference in City Hall. While sitting in the waiting room, destined to stay until audience was gained, the board member would recall his unofficial status under the weak-mayor government and speculate about the different situation that would prevail if he could turn the clock back. In those days such a trip to City Hall would have been unnecessary. One could go laterally to Selectman Dorsey or Superintendent Kane or stay on the site and make all the decisions himself.

Audience was eventually gained with the city manager, who was informed that the trucks from Fitchville were then in the process of dumping their cubic yards of gravel and that the director of Public

Works was needed at the site as soon as possible. Jay agreed to send Harold Walz without delay.

The director of Public Works and this advisor quickly sketched adequate "specs" sufficient for contractor Adelman, making provisions not only for entrances and exits but also for islets around the base of the linden trees that bordered on Mohegan Road. The theory was that the circular islets would be graded with loam and seeded, thus adding some beautification to the entire area. It was a good idea by Walz, and even before he sent his men and equipment to the site for the final grading, one could easily envisage an attractive ultimate result.

None of this was lost upon executive Etlinger when he arrived on a tour of inspection. And it was then that the manager began really to take a keen interest in the operation. No longer would the high-level considerations in the office at City Hall transcend the parking lot at Mohegan Park, and no longer would Recreation Field and associated activities continue as a poor relation. In fact, the manager made frequent trips, sometimes twice daily, and not only ordered Public Works to loam and seed the circular islets but also the bank to the east of the tennis courts, which would provide a logical and very appropriate viewing place for spectators as well as a reasonable buffer zone from the higher-elevated parking lot.

Subsequently, when the grass began to grow, one of the manager's main preoccupations was the new grass per se, which he hated to see disturbed or worn down from too much traffic of any kind—automotive or pedestrian. The new growth in the islets and on the east bank came to be known as "Etlinger's grass." At the conclusion of the project, after the grass was in clear evidence, the city manager became so enthralled with the place that he summoned photographers from the *Norwich Bulletin*, both for the purpose of exposing the parking facility and Recreation Field, and possibly to emphasize the efficiency inherent in the council-manager form of government.

While all this was a matter of interest, the important point is that once Jay Etlinger observed the possibilities and envisaged the ultimate result, he followed through. Moreover, his enthusiasm in respect to the maintenance of the grass in the islets and elsewhere had a positive impact on the entire complex with its baseball and softball fields, basketball as well as tennis courts, all of which the parking lot served. The Department of Recreation and, in the final analysis, the entire city of Norwich were then, and are now, the beneficiaries of Jay Etlinger's interest and enthusiasm.

Now Recreation Field was shaping up, on both the north and south sides of Mohegan Road. And it was well along in the process of becoming one of the best municipal recreation areas around, an asset to Norwich. The gravel parking lot has certainly fulfilled its function well over the more than two decades to the time of this writing. And though it has served for certain unintended purposes, as, for example, a convenient nocturnal parking area for adolescents and others and a place for youthful driver experts to whirl cars in circles of unbelievably short diameters on two wheels, it probably should be left as originally built with a gravel covering, replenished occasionally and maintained accordingly. If blacktopped it would reduce much-needed absorption capability during rains, and despite the fact that stones from the gravel sometimes block important drains, resulting in unwanted flooding of the courts, it is doubtful that a bituminous surface would eliminate this problem. Leaves and debris will sometimes block the drains anyway. In addition, skid marks from tires on a blacktopped surface take longer to disappear, presenting an unpleasant sight in the interim.

Courts conditioned prior to Norwich Free Academy girls' interscholastic match, November 3, 1983

Interscholastic match begins

The courts under construction, November, 1954. Note the piles of clay (from Sterling Mott's farm) and the unfinished area in front

The same view in August, 1958, showing four completed tennis courts and parking lot in front with islets of grass

Finalists from the first Southern New England Tennis Tournament, 1959. Left to right: Gerry Slobin, doubles finalist; Henri Salaun, singles winner; Richard Heath, doubles finalist; Jules Cohen, singles runner-up and doubles winner; Larry Lewis, doubles winner; Steve Armstrong, tournament chairman

Finalists from the 25th annual Southern New England Tennis Championships, 1983. Left to right: Paul Arciero, doubles winner; Joe Boquin, singles runner-up; John Arciero, doubles winner; Sasa Mahr-Batuz, singles winner and doubles runner-up; Tony Giorgetti, doubles runner-up; Steve Armstrong, tournament chairman

Angelo "Prunzie" Yeitz positioning and attaching his post straightening device

Angelo operating the jack, bending post back to perfect upright position

The author pulling a six-foot drag brush over the courts

15

The Southern New England Championships

The year following the completion of the parking lot, 1959, seven years after the installation of the council-manager form of government, was another significant one for Norwich, which was organized and incorporated 300 years earlier in 1659. The moguls of the Tercentenary Committee charged with the job of staging a fitting celebration asked this advisory board member if it would be possible to put on a special tennis event as part of the program planned for the three-hundredth anniversary of the city. It was the consensus of the brain trust that the Norwich Tennis Association, now a member of the national organization, could probably run a sanctioned tournament in conjunction with the Tercentenary celebration. Recreation Field was finally in good overall shape. In addition to the new parking area next to the tennis courts, new bleachers had been erected at the baseball field, a project initiated by this board member, then chairman of the advisory group. The main building had been spruced up and the whole establishment was presentable at long last, quite suitable for the running of a major sports event.

It occurred to one or two imaginative members of the brain trust that while many sanctioned tournaments were run by tennis clubs that comprised the New England sectional association (as many as any other section in the United States) there were none with the designation "Southern New England Tennis Championships" in adult events. Such a recognized championship would surely attract outstanding players from throughout New England and perhaps elsewhere as well. Since Norwich was ideally located in southern New England it was decided to apply for the sanction of an event with that designation. If approved, it would replace the previous tournament, the Eastern Connecticut Tennis Championships.

There was no difficulty in obtaining sanction for the new event. This advisory board member was then close to the hierarchy that controlled New England tennis, and at that time was chairman of the Membership Committee for the entire six states. Since, in its three years of existence, the eastern Connecticut tournament had the third week in August for an approved date, the brain trust wanted a better period of time for the action anyway. In a day when there were almost no outdoor lighted facilities, and few indoor courts to turn to in case of rain, it was difficult to conclude a tournament on schedule in late summer. The Tournament Committee therefore looked forward to both the new designation and the change in the scheduled date to midsummer when the evening daylight was substantially longer. The first Southern New England Tennis Championships thus took place July 9 to July 12 during the Tercentenary celebration of the city of Norwich.

Despite the difficulties involved in running the first tournament in 1959, the dedicated few who comprised the committee decided to retain the event and the new designation on a year-to-year basis. The boys could not know at the time that 1983 would record its twenty-fifth consecutive occurrence in Norwich, and in view of the obstacles encountered in concluding the first one, it's surprising there was anything left by way of stimulus or spirit to stage a subsequent tournament. It wasn't that the committee didn't know how to run this show with a larger and more formidable field of participants. Rather it was because the problems were quite different from the normal situation—in fact, singularly unique.

That first event was beset with all kinds of complications. Not the least was the fact that it was virtually impossible for the players to struggle their way through traffic jams, parades, and special events associated with the celebration and arrive at the tennis courts on schedule. Even those who had previously participated in Norwich tournaments were stymied. Few knew the back way to the courts through the winding roads of Mohegan Park, and Mahan Drive was not then in existence. Moreover, use of the two clay courts at the Home-Ec site was ruled out because of the difficulties involved in driving within reasonable distance of the area, since the nearby Chelsea parade was the focal point for most of the special events. The ones who did succeed in making it were obliged to wait interminably before they could drive out across Broadway. The West Side Tennis Court on Forest Street, still maintained by Ted Montgomery, was utilized, but those who were led to his private court were seldom seen again the same day. Enough matches were played there, however, to be of real assistance to the Tournament Committee, and without its availability the first Southern New England Championships might have gone on for the balance of the summer. The field was so large that the four municipal courts at Mohegan Park were simply not adequate.

Also, there were scheduled functions conceived by the Tercentenary Committee right in that new parking lot next to the tennis courts—for example, log-dragging competition by teams of working horses. To say that these adjacent activities were distracting to the players is the classic understatement in southern New England tennis history. It is truly amazing that the events, Men's Singles and Men's Doubles, were finished within the contemplated time span. At the conclusion the chairman made the following profound observation: he would never run a tennis tournament in conjunction with a tercentenary celebration again. A safe enough statement.

The twenty-four subsequent tournaments, 1960 to 1983 inclusive, though far from easy to run, were not so complicated. One is reminded here of a comment by Henri Salaun, who once said that no one knows what's involved in running a tournament until he does it once. How Henri would qualify his observation if the sanctioned events are run as part of municipal celebrations of the magnitude of the Tercentenary is an easy speculation. If there's no way for the players, after arriving in town, to get to the premises, this situation does not add to the smoothness with which the show can proceed.

The Tercentenary over, the Southern New Englands established on a permanent basis, the brain trust annually turned to the task of running the subsequent tournaments. Committee members could not know in 1959 that over the next two decades more than 10,000 new tennis balls would be thrown out to competitors for their confrontations, that over 2,500 tournament matches would be played in this tourney alone on the unscreened clay from Sterling Mott's farm in Coventry and the integrated mixture of clay from Asylum Avenue in Hartford and gravel from Norwich banks. Neither could they know the extent to which the sports event would attract top-ranking tennis players in New England as well as participants who hailed from such faraway places as Colombia, New Zealand, Hawaii, and Japan. The list of entries has also included players from many colleges. At one time or another every Ivy League school has been represented, and captains of the teams at such tennis powerhouses as Ohio State, the University of Texas, and the University of Miami have participated. In recent years the tournament has drawn heavily from the New York City area—for example, Steve Stockton from Garden City, who now resides in Norwich; the well-known Barrow brothers (Doug and John); and Steve Ross, the tennis player written up in the *New York Times* as having on one occasion out-hustled Bobby Riggs.

While the story of the Southern New England Championships is far from the fundamental theme in this recounting, it is not irrelevant to stay with it a little longer. It is important to take note of citizen involvement and to pay tribute to those Norwich residents who have opened their homes to house the tournament players. Needless to say, the committee in charge of arranging the housing, chaired for many years by Anna Fuery, deserves equal accolades also. All this has had much to do with the popularization of the tournament and much to do with its success. And there have been some interesting, unanticipated developments. Steve Stockton, for example, former number-one player at the University of Oklahoma and Big Eight tennis champion, no doubt would not have settled in Norwich were it not for the Southern New Englands. He was housed near the courts at the home of George and Beverly Silverman, where he met his future wife, Diane.

There have been other substantial contributions by interested citizens of Norwich. For many years these people made and provided sandwiches for the players gratuitously. It is important to take note of the late John Martin's family, whose contributions go far beyond any words that can be written. The doctor's daughters, Nancy, Susie, Kathy, and Janie, organized the solicitation, and there were many times that the Martin home was a virtual assembly line for quick production. Not only was this appreciated by the participants, who didn't have to go out and buy their lunch somewhere, but also this service helped the committee no end. It is important in an accelerated tournament such as the Southern New Englands to keep the players at or near the courts so they'll be available when needed. No one could ever know for certain when the boys might return after going, purportedly, to a downtown or other restaurant. If it has happened once it has happened a hundred times: a player will stalk the chairman half the day inquiring as to when he'll be getting on the courts for his next match, and when the time comes when his presence is really necessary, he has, for all practical purposes, disappeared from the surface of the earth. Virtually all of them, theoretically, were at a restaurant for lunch. It is easy to see that the sandwiches were almost indispensable in those days. Things are different now since arrangements have been made so that lunch may be purchased at the courts.

Over much of the more than two decades of the Southern New Englands, however, some of our people in Norwich have made contributions on this score quite beyond that of sandwich making, notably those of Dr. and Mrs. Fred Eadie, who have held many cookouts for the tournament players and tennis friends—usually on Friday evenings of the weekend events. And no couple really knows what's involved in putting on such a spread or what the tab amounts to in satiating the appetites of about a hundred hungry tennis players until they do it once. The same could be said of the Saturday night buffet at the Tournament Committee chairman's house that has traditionally followed the Eadie cookout. The offerings of many volunteer cooks who have contributed their "specialty" have added to the variety and copiousness of the "spreads."

But it's all been well worth the effort and expenditure, for many are the friendships that have been established. This holds for those who have housed out-of-town participants as well, and in all cases the hospitality has been such that substantial breakfasts have been provided for the players each morning. In Norwich, as in many places elsewhere, the guests have received preferential treatment, which has been genuinely appreciated. Many are those, having played here once or twice, who ask to be housed with the same hosts of the previous year when they file their entries. Such has been the case in respect to the former long-time sports editor of the *Norwich Bulletin*, Tim Tolokan, and his wife, who have not only housed many players over the years but also have helped out in other ways as well. About the only thing that Mr. Tolokan, whose coverage of the tournament has been excellent and worthy of a New England Association award, did not do is house the Harvard student tennis player who once ate six eggs and a half-pound of bacon for breakfast in the chairman's home.

Perhaps enough has now been said about the Southern New England Tennis Championships to establish conclusively that it has not been a show staged by the Tournament Committee alone. Yet there are still other accolades to be made, for no word has been written in respect to the contributions of the players themselves. Some have embellished the tournament simply by virtue of their presence—in particular, Henri Salaun, for many years New England's number-one-ranking player. The committee will never forget his fine statement, one year when he received the winner's trophy, that the tournament in Norwich was the strongest in New England that year. (Henri, of course, was referring only to the New England circuit and not the national and international events at Longwood in Brookline, Massachusetts, and Newport, Rhode Island.) But Mr. Salaun has made contributions equal to if not greater than his comments. One of the world's great athletes in his prime—four times national squash rackets champion, and in 1954 the world open champion, while at the same time being New England's number-one-ranking tennis player for so many years—Henri always put on a superb and crowd-pleasing show. Spectators who were privileged here to watch Salaun in person have frequently commented that they'd rather watch Henri on a clay court than anyone else on this planet.

As previously indicated, it is not the purpose here to write a comprehensive history of the southern New England tournament. Rather, it is meant simply to point out the caliber of the players attracted to the makeshift Norwich complex. Perhaps, if they had known of the presence of the innumerable stones from municipal gravel banks in the surface proper, covered only with granular top dressing, many would not have shown up. Obviously, others besides Henri Salaun have come to play and vie for the title. One who comes to mind immediately is Jules Cohen of Rhode Island. Once a New England champion while still a Yale undergraduate, regarded by many as the best doubles player in the region at his prime and having ranked as high as number two in the six-state area in singles, Jules happily was a consistent performer here for many years. In the early 1960s he and Henri Salaun played perhaps the most memorable match in the history of the finals of the Southern New Englands. Salaun prevailed in the days before the tie breaker 15-13—6-3, 6-4. There were only three breaks of service in the entire match, in the first set not until the twenty-seventh game.

There followed a period of a few years dominated largely by Jim Biggs of Southport, Connecticut—a true sportsman, athlete, gentleman, and friend. A former Eastern Intercollegiate champion while at Dartmouth, Jim has won more titles, singles and doubles combined, than anyone else in the history of the tournament. Then came the era of Ted Hoehn, former New England champion and number-one-ranking player in the entire section, and a very special person regarded with high esteem here and elsewhere. Ted now runs the Windridge Tennis Camp in Jeffersonville, Vermont.

Having gone this far, it is important to name others. As in the case of those already mentioned, the order in which they come to mind is neither chronological nor does it relate to arbitrary comparative tennis prowess or otherwise. They are all of equal status in every respect and all, by virtue of their presence and participation, have made significant contributions to the Southern New England Tennis Championships. Also, it's important to pay tribute to those whose names do not appear here, for their entries have been equally valued and their contributions equally pertinent. Tournaments, at least those held on the gravel-and-clay-composition courts in Norwich, are not designed for the aggrandizement of the topnotchers exclusively in either the men's or women's divisions, the latter being added to the tournament schedule in 1966.

The expansion of the Southern New Englands, encompassing women's competition along with the men's, has not only enlarged the tournament but also has stimulated interest, with the happy result that a truly legitimate and all-inclusive event was established on a permanent basis. The enhancement of the field to include women coincided both with the increase in experience of the Tournament Committee and the growing emphasis assigned to women's sports activities. Norwich's own Dorothy O'Neil, former national badminton champion, won the first three southern New England tennis titles in 1966, 1967, and 1968.

Would that time, space, and effort were sufficient to name the well over 1,000 separate individuals who have played in this event, but suffice it to say that of the many complimentary letters the committee has received after each tournament, just as many have come from first- and second-round losers as from those who have taken home the trophies. Perhaps enough has been expressed along these lines to explain away the natural tendency to list winners, runners-up and high-ranking players. And so, without taking anything away from the many other participants, here goes.

The amazing Ned Weld, former Harvard star and twelve times the winner of the New England Tennis Championships, prevailed here in the early 1960s. Other champions during this decade were Sam Schoonmaker, a former Yale captain and recent president of the New England Lawn Tennis Association; previously mentioned Steve Stockton, now of Norwich, winner in 1966; and personable Charlie Hoeveler, erstwhile Dartmouth star. Charlie has won both the New England doubles championship (with Jim Biggs in 1969) and the New England intercollegiate title in singles.

The popular Bob Kiniry of New Britain, Connecticut, won the tournament in 1973. Bob's victory was the highlight of his career, and he will be the first one to say that this was his most significant triumph in tennis. The field was very strong that year and included such formidable players as Bill Drake and team captain Miller of Brown University. Other champions in the men's division who emerged around that time were Steve Ross, previously mentioned conqueror of Bobby Riggs, and Graham Snook of New Zealand. Graham, who was a student at the University of Southern Illinois at the time, elected to make the circuit throughout much of the United States that summer, including the New Englands in Boston and the Southern New Englands in Norwich on his schedule. Both of these tournaments were won by the New Zealander.

The astute Doug Teetor from Ridgefield, Connecticut, former Cornell University star, won the championship in 1975, and at the top of his tennis agenda is that of taking the title once more. The following year was very interesting when three Japanese Davis Cuppers entered the event: Sochio Kato, Takao Yammamoto, and Nobuya Tamura. Kato, who at the time ranked number four in Japan, won the tournament, defeating one of the East's better players, Joe Booquin of Danbury, Connecticut, in the finals. Booquin had gained the title round by virtue of a semifinal win over Yammamoto in one of the best matches ever played in Norwich, 6-4, 4-6, 6-4.

Phil Kadesch of Winchester, Massachusetts, a talented player with an ATP computer ranking (Association of Tennis Professionals) and who ranked number one in New England in 1982, dominated the competition in recent years, winning in 1977, 1979, 1980, and 1981. His victory skein was interrupted only once, in 1978, a year in which the lithe left-hander did not participate. The 1978 tournament was won by Dr. Harold German of New York City. The doctor, who returned to competitive play after a few years' absence, before which he ranked as high as number six in the Eastern Sectional Association, was highly pleased with his return to form and his victory here. Bud Schultz of Meriden, Connecticut, and a fine intercollegiate basketball player at Bates, won the 1982 tournament. The current title-holder is Sasa Mahr Batuz, an exciting acrobatic young player who was born and brought up in Argentina. Sasa has been in the United States about six years now.

Competition in the women's division has been equally intense over the years and has included many top-ranking players, among them internationally known Beth Norton of Fairfield, Connecticut, whose game later progressed to the point where she nearly defeated

Virginia Wade of Great Britain, 1977 Wimbledon champion, in a long three-set match, played here. As a young teenager she surprised everyone by gaining the semifinals, where she lost to top-seeded and eventual winner of the tournament, Ann Murphy of East Hartford. Andrea Voikos of Pawtucket, Rhode Island, whose devastating ground strokes almost placed her in a class by herself in those days, won the Southern New Englands twice in the early 1970s. And the talented Una Keyes of Westwood, Massachusetts, who later was to play with the Boston Lobsters, also prevailed on two occasions later on in the seventies. In more recent years the tournament has been dominated by Heather Eldredge of Groton Long Point, Connecticut, and Cheryl Dow of Manchester, Connecticut. The remarkable Miss Eldredge first won the Southern New Englands in 1979 without the loss of even one set at the unbelievable age of thirteen. She returned in 1981 when she again captured the title, but this time after a hard-fought three-set battle with Cheryl Dow. Miss Dow, a student at William and Mary College, where she compiled a fine intercollegiate record, won the tournament again in 1982. The current title-holder is Robin Boss of Rhode Island, now a student at Harvard. Miss Boss is a very agile, steady player, who until the 1983 season had been a high-ranking junior.

Some others who come to mind who have played consistently in the Southern New Englands are Gerry Slobin of Hartford, several times Connecticut's highest-ranking player and former captain of the University of Miami; the amazing Peter Vieira of Newington, Connecticut, top-ranked New England senior player whose game has improved with the years (Peter first gained a New England ranking in the top ten of the regular men's division after becoming a junior veteran, the age thirty-five and over category); Mary Wisnieski of Warren, Rhode Island, who won the women's title in 1969; Ginny Gilbane Mahoney, former national top-ranking junior, who won the same event in 1974; Gayle Goodburn of Rutland, Vermont, who was thrilled to win the championship in 1975; Eve Ellis of Yale University, who prevailed in 1978; Phil Coons of Glastonbury, Connecticut, who reached the men's finals in 1978 after more than seven hours of competitive play the previous day; Ben Bishop, then of Duxbury, Massachusetts, and now a teaching professional in the Hartford area, who was the champion in 1970; and former football player Jack Redmond, one-time University of Connecticut quarterback, who was a recent title-holder in men's doubles with Phil Coons.

We'll now leave this brief history of some of the participants in the Southern New England Tennis Championships and return to the story of the gravel and clay championship courts subsequent to the Tercentenary.

16

Tennis Courts at the Pautipaug Country Club

The main task now was simply that of keeping abreast of maintenance problems with which we had become thoroughly accustomed.

But this was to be complicated somewhat by virtue of a new development, for the years 1960 and 1961 saw this advisory board member become chairman of the Tennis Committee at a private country club, then in the process of construction. Something of the story of this involvement is a necessary departure because of some secondary, beneficial impacts on certain structural aspects of the Mohegan Park complex as well as its complementary function in respect to tennis activity in the area generally.

By then some reputation had been established, one supposes, and if something was going on by way of tennis development, it was only natural to exhibit interest and even offer assistance. Perhaps if the directors of this club off Pautipaug Hill in the adjacent town of Sprague were familiar with the real story of the municipal courts with the preponderance of stones in the surface and fence posts from junk yards, the advisory board member might not have been asked to serve as chairman of the Tennis Committee. Some of the facts about the courts at Recreation Field were hardly in keeping with the sophistication of a private country club.

But this proposition represented a different sort of challenge, and this time the chairman's function would be truly advisory and administrative. It would be totally unlike developments subsequent to the meeting in the mayor's office in 1950. Answers to such basic questions as to what would be the most appropriate surface and the best location for the complex on the premises would be resolved intelligently; specifications would be forthcoming, put out for bid; and adequate funds would be available to award the contract accordingly.

After attending a few meetings, however, it was apparent that such was not to be the case, that the club was financially tight at the time, and had difficulty getting off the ground. A land corporation had been formed, sufficient acreage had been acquired for a picturesque golf course, which had been substantially completed by the time the advisory board member became involved. The major decisions had been made by then. It was to be a family-type club with a swimming pool, tennis courts, snack bar, dining room, locker and shower facilities, and so on. But at this stage there were doubting Thomases in view of the astronomical projects that remained. And many wanted to bide time before putting up the necessary $1,000 for the required bond.

It was apparent furthermore that tennis was still the poor relation, and that we were in a situation roughly comparable to that at Recreation Field in Mohegan Park a decade earlier. If courts were to arrive upon the scene at the Pautipaug Country Club, the procedure therein adopted would of necessity be a far cry from a modern or scientific approach—setting up specifications and putting them out for bid, and so forth. And Chairman Alfred Maurer of the Sports and Pastime Committee, after learning something of the cost entailed in building courts if awarded to tennis court building contractors, soon decided that the only hope was to proceed as the city of Norwich did at Mohegan Park. He then asked this member of his committee if he would consider proceeding accordingly.

Why not? Perhaps it would be a more prestigious effort and accomplishment in some ways. And everybody likes status with the business and professional wheels. Moreover, there'd be far greater direct control and no bother with routines and intricacies of the council-manager form of government or disabled equipment. In addition, there would be some funds to work with this time.

Some tennis friends wondered why one who had knocked himself out in connection with public facilities would do the same thing for a private club. "You're not a country club guy," one of them remarked. While he was definitely right in the long term, he wasn't in the short. Tennis was really growing at that point in time and more facilities were needed to take the load off the city courts. Also, there was valuable experience and know-how to be gained by virtue of tackling a new complex, public or private, all of which adds to one's education. And it is herein and forthwith laid down that the effort entailed in building tennis courts gratuitously for a private country club adds profoundly to one's education—particularly in the erstwhile cow pastures of Sprague.

The first decision to be made was that of selecting the site. It would be undesirable to build the courts too close to either snack bar or swimming pool. The tennis chairman knew from experience, having observed similar situations elsewhere, that there'd be too much noise and distraction. While four courts would be the ultimate goal and minimum requirement for the estimated membership, it was decided to build just two courts for the time being (two more could always be added in the future) on the side hill north of Dow's Lane, the road leading to the club—some 200 yards from the swimming pool and clubhouse area. It was the former cow pasture adjacent to the backyard of farmer Bushnell, from whom the land was purchased. There was just about enough space between the tee and fairway of the dogleg par four twelfth hole and the property line to the east for two batteries of two courts each headed north-south end to end. (Some golfers would have the capability of slicing their drives from the tee onto the tennis courts, it turned out, but this was a difficult stroke and happened very rarely.)

How two tennis courts emerged on this wet site, while not one of the seven wonders of all time, at a cost well under $5,000, is positively amazing. Although not the purpose here to write that story, its main significance being the impact on the tennis situation and complex in Norwich, some of the difficulties involved may be of interest. The rich black loam, which had to be stripped, was the richest ever produced by the combined efforts of nature, man, and animal. When turned over by bulldozer the cow manure stench was pervasive beyond description. Moreover, as the golfers who trudge the twelfth fairway know, the site is about the wettest on planet earth—even in periods of drought. There's a claylike hard-pan base under topsoil and subsoil that precludes penetration of moisture. (The Indian name of Pautipaug denotes "a boggy meadow.") Even the dozers got stranded in the muck and to the point where they had to be pulled out by another transported to the site on a low-bed. A standby bulldozer, for example, was required to be on hand to haul out the trucks that delivered ready mixed concrete for swimming pool construction after they dumped their loads. There was no other way they could get out for the next trip.

In the spring of 1961 the Pautipaug Country Club was an implausible spectacle, to say the very least. Those, such as the late Ted Mallon—the club's first president, who envisaged an ultimate well-groomed clubhouse, swimming pool, and tennis complex, are to be credited with both optimism and imagination. Gigantic piles of topsoil and subsoil were in evidence everywhere. The artesian well diggers were pounding endlessly into the earth in search of water; there was plenty of it on the surface of the terrain but no more until a long way below it. No wonder potential members, the doubting Thomases, adopted a wait-and-see attitude. And had it not been for the previous experiences at Recreation Field, when at times everything looked hopeless, the chairman of the Tennis Committee might well have turned away too, for it was necessary to proceed in much the same manner as in the park, crossing bridges somehow when you got to them, this time on the slimy terrain of the remote cow pastures of Sprague.

But this advisory board-country club tennis chairman stuck with the assignment, and happily so, for he soon became the recipient of two distinct lucky breaks. The chairman will accept some credit for the first one but not the second. After the rich black loam was stripped by Dave Geer's heavy bulldozers and pushed into a huge pile at the lower north side, and after the exposed terrain was eventually leveled by the powerful machines, it was obvious that tennis courts could not emerge on the site unless a legitimate base was somehow established. A sand and gravel contractor, George Caviggia, whose bank was not far from Pautipaug Hill Road, was then engaged to bring in over 1,000 cubic yards of gravel to provide an adequate base for the courts. The cost was about one dollar per yard. Operating with one truck, and by himself from dawn to dusk, the contractor was able to deliver the requisite volume and spread same over the muddy area in a few days.

Because of some of the unexpected difficulties more funds had now been committed than anticipated. The 450-foot-long-by-12-foot-high rectangular fence was then in the process of construction, arrangements having been made with contractor Tom Fitzpatrick. And the heaviest expenditures were yet to be made. The volume of material to be applied over Caviggia's gravel appeared unattainable. At the very minimum, about 4,000 cubic feet, or roughly 150 cubic yards of appropriate material, preferably clay, would be needed. The tennis chairman had really stuck his neck out this time. There would be little chance even of obtaining the required material, let alone the honing and grading for a satisfactory surface.

Then came the first lucky break. We had been looking at a partial answer to the problem all along. It was at the swimming pool site where in digging out the base for the pool the contractor had run into deep layers of yellow subsoil, or silt. This material, at least 20 percent clay and a better grade than used at the West Side Tennis Court on Forest Street a quarter of a century earlier, was simply lying there nearby in a huge pile.

The late Henry Lebejko, a contractor with light equipment, was engaged to transport 150 cubic yards of this silt to the tennis court site where it was graded to perfection by hired personnel (mostly college students) as though for the final playing surface. At the worst, we could now come up with something, for the subsoil from the pool area, by itself, was sufficient in quality for a mediocre tennis facility, assuming use of calcium chloride in substantial quantity. But for a better result, the integration of legitimate clay was needed.

Lebejko was sent to the Middletown source to get about thirty cubic yards of brickyard clay, which was distributed over the subsoil base. The proposition now was to integrate this clay somehow with that base. If troweled in or done otherwise by hand, no one would know in which decade the courts would be ready for play. Then came the second lucky break.

Somewhere about this point in the process of speculation it was observed by Henry Lebejko and his operator that the metal belt conveyors that propelled his payloader might be ideal for driving the clay into the subsoil base if the machine was run back and forth over the surface. The weight of the vehicle turned out to be just right for the job and the process of integrating the clay with the material that once resided in the swimming pool was completed in short order—involving no more than a couple of hours. Moreover, the two-court complex, the base having been carefully leveled and pitched by hand tools, emerged almost perfect, a 120-foot-by-105-foot flawless plane. Once the difficult preliminary work was done, no tennis courts were ever completed as quickly, and except for the embellishments such as setting the net posts, putting down the linseed-oil-and-traffic-paint lines, and applying the ground-slate top dressing together with some calcium chloride, the two-court country club complex was a fait accompli. It was opened for play on July 7, 1961, the day that the third Southern New England Tennis Championships began at Mohegan Park.

The number-one-seeded player, Henri Salaun, was already in town, as was another top seed, Larry Lewis, who ranked well up in New England's top ten. Henri, having received a first-round bye, was not scheduled to play that Thursday evening, and he was somewhat disappointed since he wanted to limber up and get a workout. He even asked the tournament chairman to take some time out and play a set or so, but the four courts were continually in use for the other matches and the director was preoccupied as well. However, a possible answer came quickly to mind. How about the new courts at the country club, just finished earlier that day? It was a good idea, particularly since the chairman really was interested in reactions and commentaries as to their playability. No one would be better on this score than Henri, who was agreeable to the plan. The next proposition was that of finding an appropriate opponent for the top-seeded performer. The chairman was too busy running the show and, moreover, was simply not a good enough tennis player to give Henri much of a workout. But Larry Lewis then was leaving the courts after completing a comparatively easy first-round match, and he was pleased with the suggestion that he play Henri a couple of sets of tennis on the new courts at the country club. It was necessary to take some time out from the tournament and lead the way to Pautipaug. At least as much time would be required to spell out directions as to drive the eight-mile circuitous route and have them follow. The two participants, who for a while thought they had been conned into a fictitious escapade, were relieved to find that there were in fact tennis courts at the conclusion of the drive.

The chairman stayed for a while to watch with interest a few games of the first match to be played there. It was interesting furthermore that this confrontation involved two of New England's best. Farmer Bushnell, who was raking up some debris in his adjacent backyard, was the one other spectator. But he was an intermittent onlooker. It was obvious when one looked in his direction and observed him go back to work immediately that he didn't enjoy being caught watching such an implausible, unproductive activity, whatever it might be. That he was in close proximity of a show equally as good as there would be in the Southern New Englands that year, or any other year, made no difference. He had more important things to do.

After the tennis match, won by Salaun, and after the contestants somehow found their way back to Mohegan Park on their own, they were soon questioned by the chairman as to what they thought of the country club complex. Surprisingly, they had no complaints relative to the surface, and they felt that it would improve with subsequent play and appropriate maintenance. But they did have difficulty with the background. In an area with no trees or foliage to the west or north, and only large tall ones to the south on Dow's Lane, visibility was poor—particularly from the north end. The bank to the road provided good background up to about one-third of the twelve-foot fence, but beyond that there was a void, and it was hard to see the tennis ball when viewed coming out of open space. Now you see it; now you don't. And even from the south, visibility was not much better; far distant hills reaching up to a fairly high horizon sufficed for what there was. Also, it is easy to surmise that it was a very windy place with no protection from foliage in an elevated area.

The tennis chairman decided to do something about all this. It took a few years to do it, but arborvitae trees were planted on the west side of the complex, and these tough evergreens have done their job well in reducing the impact of the prevailing winds across the open ninth and twelfth fairways. But the arborvitae to the west couldn't help the background to the north or south. However, tennis court suppliers by then had come up with products that would readily solve such problems. Reference is made to shade curtains, sometimes called wind screens, whose primary function is precisely that of improving background and visibility. They have the further capability of reducing the impact of disturbing winds. All are designed to allow penetration of air; otherwise neither the curtains nor the fences could handle the pressure from gale-force turbulence.

It was an easy bill of goods to sell the then president of the club, Bill Harding, and forthwith two huge saran curtains were purchased to be hung on the fences at the north and south ends. Each was 100 feet in length and 8 feet in width. Thus the background problem was solved, and in short order. The tennis chairman did not know, however, that the purported solution to the problem would not be permanent, that the shade curtain background was destined to be shortlived, for he had made a colossal error.

The story is simply that it was a mistake to order curtains of that dimension, 100 feet by 8 feet, or 800 square feet. Despite the fact that they are designed to allow a certain amount of air to penetrate through them, such large curtains represent a tremendous barrier in high winds, particularly in an unprotected area such as Pautipaug. Needless to say, the fences couldn't withstand the pressure, and when the first heavy wind came along from the south the fence posts were bent to an angle approaching forty-five degrees relative to the level of the courts. All of which presented an unaesthetic sight at the country club.

It also presented a serious problem for the chairman who was in another real bind. Brand-new two-inch black iron pipe, painted green, had been used for the fence posts, whose life expectancy should have been in the range of decades rather than weeks, and here they were damaged irreparably. A half-dozen or so adult tennis players were mobilized first to remove the shade curtains from the fences and then to endeavor to push the posts into place. But the posts would spring right back to the previous angular position. Somebody suggested tying a rope to the top of each post and attaching the other end to a truck, which would then pull the pipe back into an upright position again. But such a procedure would no doubt result in bending the posts in additional places. The only curve in the hitherto straight pipe was immediately above the footings at ground level, and it would be unwise to introduce more.

Without question there was an answer to the problem while salvaging the posts at the same time. But any conceivable solution, such as dismantling the fence, straightening the posts by applying heat at the bend points, perhaps, and rebuilding, would be major and expensive. Speculation continued, however, to no avail, until the chairman sought the advice of Angelo "Prunzie" Yeitz, a municipal employee who worked for the Police Department. Maintenance of the parking meters and the posts to which they were attached was one of Prunzie's assignments. He was an experienced hand at straightening bent meter posts that were hit by automobiles, whose drivers frequently failed to maneuver their vehicles into the parking places without contact with the uprights.

Prunzie, in fact, had designed and made a gadget to facilitate the operation of restoring bent meter posts back to their original position. After a quick look at the fence problem at the Pautipaug tennis courts, he was certain that the posts and attached fencing could be brought back to their previous state with his equipment in a comparatively short time. Prunzie did the job, gratuitously, in one evening after work, both the north and south ends, and his workmanship was such that no one, unless he had seen the toppled fence, would ever have known that it had been the victim of gale-force winds. Thus what once appeared to be a major and almost insurmountable task was resolved in nothing flat, and all for free.

Prunzie's post-straightening device is simple, yet ingenious. A heavy steel rod, diameter about one and one-quarter inches, was cut and welded into the shape of a thirty-by-sixty-degree right triangle. The hypotenuse measures approximately twenty-eight inches, the long leg of the triangle about twenty-five inches, and the short one about fifteen. Its weight is about thirty pounds or so. The short leg of the triangular device is attached to the bent fence post just above the footing. The long leg extends beyond the vertex of the ninety-degree angle, and the extension contains a U-shaped clamp, which is securely bolted to the post fifteen inches above the top of the footing. The hypotenuse extends beyond the vertex at the other end of the short leg in the form of a rugged hook, which is curled around the post at the very top of the footing. The short leg is thus secured to the post with the hook at the bottom where the post is bent. The triangle is perpendicular to the ground, the hypotenuse being on the down side and its intersection with the long leg, or acute vertex, extending out twenty-five inches from the post. A simple hand-operated hydraulic jack is then placed under the acute vertex, which is specially designed so that the lifting mechanism won't slip off. A few hand-operated vertical strokes with the handle of the jack and up goes the fence post back to its original position. The leverage created is amazing.

Needless to say, the 800-square-foot saran shade curtains were not reinstalled on the fences in the same manner. But there was still the problem with the open-space background. After analyzing the situation, however, it was observed that narrower curtains would be equally effective. As indicated, when looking south the background was adequate to the level of Dow's Lane, and therefore all that was needed was to provide something from that point on up. A curtain 4 feet in width would be sufficient to fill in this critical area. Moreover, in view of the substantially reduced wind resistance factor, there would be far less strain on the fences. Also, the smaller curtain would not be awkward, would be easier to install, and the appearance of the whole complex would be improved. And all of this applied to the south end as well.

Without further speculation we had the curtains cut in half locally, by Marty Gilman, Inc., and new grommets inserted on the appropriate sides. This operation turned out to be less difficult and expensive than anticipated, and the club wound up with four shade curtains instead of two. The additional ones were used on the next courts to the south, which were built subsequently. The curtains were taken down each fall, for it was a certainty that otherwise the fence posts would not withstand the rough winds of the winter months.

Everything went along without incident for a few years until one late August morning when wind gusts of hurricane force from tropical storm Doria caused havoc at the club. Trees and telephone poles went down as well as the north and south fences of the now four-court tennis complex. The arborvitae trees to the west survived and the shade curtains themselves were intact, remaining secured to their respective fences, which were bent thirty-five to forty degrees. The winds didn't appear that severe, but one major gust did the damage, and that is all it takes. And even then the fences could have survived unscathed had the wind struck obliquely. But Doria came in perpendicularly at a perfect ninety degrees and the iron fence posts couldn't take it.

However, by nightfall on that same day the posts were upright once again, thanks to a fast trip to the Norwich Police Department to borrow Prunzie's straightener one more time. The job was done without removing the shade curtains, too, so that when the day's work was concluded that Saturday the tennis courts looked the same as before the advent of the tropical storm. It took public utilities and Southern New England Telephone a little longer.

The availability of Prunzie's device was probably crucial given the relative status of the racket game at the club, for otherwise the cost to rebuild the fences would be such that the tennis court area might well have been bulldozed once more, this time for a parking lot. At the nineteenth-hole executive sessions the subject was brought up many times, even though facetiously. There was other good-natured ribbing that was thoroughly enjoyed both by orator and audience, and for the most part by the tennis chairman also, who had been labeled the "sweaty tennisean." The designation was ascribed by Herbert Warren Bruce Sidney Farr, top executive at Plastic Wire and Cable Corporation. Upon returning to the clubhouse for a shower after tennis, a stentorian voice would resound throughout the place. "There's a stench in this locker room. Tell that tennisean to take a good hot shower, then send him to the lounge for a drink, but have him sit at the end of the bar. . . . Put it on my tab."

The executive vice-president was really an asset to tennis and the program at the country club. His gibes and good-natured horseplay accentuated the existence of the game at the club, for Mr. Farr knew more than his kidding might imply, and he was quite aware of the history of the courts as well as the problems encountered. He knew, for instance, that tennis players for nine years carried water from the clubhouse in a five-gallon cooler for drinking purposes. Other golfers knew this also because on hot days, when at the twelfth tee, they would cross over to the courts and help themselves.

Club executives, cognizant of the water problem, had made two futile attempts designed to solve it. A well point (nothing but a pipe driven into the ground by a sledgehammer) was tried in several places, but no water was found. Then a backhoe was sent to the area to dig a hole for a shallow ten-foot well nearby in the cow pasture terrain. Circular concrete culvert-type sections were installed with a nineteenth-century hand pump on top. The water was obtained all right, but the tennis chairman had sense enough to have it tested frequently at the University of Connecticut where analysis showed conclusively that the water was "unfit for human consumption." It was poison. One foolproof way to solve the tennis problem on a permanent basis. Poison all the players.

When informed of the results of the tests, the masterminds of the executive board, which included M.D.s, insisted that the quality of the water would improve with time and use. They suggested that we keep pumping away daily for a while and the liquid would soon be fit to drink. But all subsequent tests showed no improvement whatsoever, and thus the tennis chairman kept the hand pump locked by chain and padlock. It remained so for many years—except for intermittent use of the water for other-than-drinking purposes.

The problem was eventually solved, however, on the strength of a long letter to club president Michael Conway, dated September 12, 1969. Judge Conway authorized the running of a water line from the main artesian well near the clubhouse to the tennis courts—something the chairman had asked for many times. Contractor Joe Carboni did the job in one day with his backhoe, and at a cost substantially less than the sum of the expenditures of previous efforts.

With a legitimate water supply established at long last, tennis was beginning to emerge from its timeworn poor-relation status. It had been a "long row to hoe" at the club just as in the case of the public courts at Mohegan Park. The original assumption that things might be easier at a private establishment proved to be false, the struggle for tennis equally difficult. But there were some beneficial results quite outside the many enjoyable evening hours spent in play with tennis friends. There was not only the gain in experience and know-how. The effort was worth it if for no other reason than that otherwise we wouldn't have known much about fences and loop caps and Prunzie's post-straightening gadget. We didn't know at the time of tropical storm Doria that there'd be one more major assignment for Prunzie's device. But not at the country club.

17

Top Rail on Fences at Armstrong Courts

The absence of a top rail on the tennis court fences at Mohegan Park has been mentioned a few times. Also it has been implied that one day such an embellishment would take place. The courts at the country club were enclosed by satisfactory twelve-foot fencing, the framework of which included an inch-and-a-quarter top rail attached to two-inch posts utilizing conventional loop caps. Brand-new black iron pipe, subsequently painted green, had been used. The fences at the city courts were built piecemeal in stages, and there was no top rail connecting the posts from the junk yards. If an advisory board member could somehow manage such an acceptable structure at a private club, why not at a public facility? The attainment of a better-looking fence in the conspicuous tennis area in the park had always been a matter of high concern—and not simply from the standpoint of looks, or aesthetic appearance. The welded-wire fabric attached to the posts would hang better and last longer if also suspended from a top rail. Moreover, if shade curtains were to be installed on the north fence, still another contemplated project for some time in the future, such a connector would be indispensable.

An event that occurred at the courts one day the first week of November 1967 added considerable stimulus to the idea of doing something about the fences. Earlier that year, on August 7, the Norwich

City Council had adopted a resolution naming the municipal clay courts after this advisory board member, and the dedication took place on Friday, November 3. The resolution introduced by the president pro tempore, James J. Quarto, and nicely drawn up by corporation counsel Orrin Carashick called for the director of Public Works to "provide a suitable plaque and to install same at an appropriate location at said tennis courts." Apprehension lest the Public Works director contemplate attachment of something between a couple of these junk yard fence posts added further stimulus to the idea of improving the existing setup. Concern herein was shortlived, however, for one day prior to the dedication date, while playing some tennis with Mildred Savage, author of the well-known best-selling novel *Parrish*, we observed a Public Works truck approaching the courts carrying a fairly good-sized boulder and soon depositing the mass of rock in front of the courts close to Mohegan Road. The plaque would be secured to an even, smooth face of the selected boulder and with tombstone cement!

The idea of dedicating the courts in the name of the advisory board member first started to the mind of the president pro tempore that year after he'd observed much of the Southern New England Tennis Championships. Having been interested and active in sports and recreation both prior to and during his terms on the council, Alderman Quarto well remembered the situation "back when." His introduction of the fine resolution naming the facilities will not be forgotten by at least one individual so long as he lives.

Very probably it was fortunate that Jim Quarto was able to take some time out to observe the activity during midsummer when everything was shipshape and looked pretty good. Otherwise the idea of naming the courts might not have come to mind. At that time of year the makeshift fence blended into a green background of trees and foliage and the unimposing structure did not stand out. But this was not the case at the time of the dedication. Most of the leaves by then had fallen, the place was a comparative mess, and there was no green background into which the decrepit fence could blend. Everyone knows that many facilities understandably do not look the same in late fall as in summer months, but this observation doesn't, and shouldn't, apply to a fence. While no one of the small group of spectators, which happily included Judge and Mrs. Allyn L. Brown, both well into their eighties, made any remarks or comments in respect to the unattractive fencing, the advisory board member was somewhat embarrassed, nonetheless. He was also frustrated, for there was no way, apparently, that even a reasonably decent-looking fence could be achieved without ripping out the existing improvised structure and starting from scratch. What could be done with the junk yard posts of different diameter, variation in height, and far out of line? It was not that the footings were out of line; rather the iron posts extended upward at different angles, many of the concrete foundations having been disturbed by heavy frosts.

Clearly here was one more important assignment for Prunzie's straightening device, which could easily line the uprights satisfactorily. But there were additional problems, since the posts were of different lengths and diameter. However, contractor Lebejko could see no difficulty in rectifying this situation. He would use a conventional pipe cutter to attain an even height, insert sleeves in the larger posts, and couple appropriate pieces to the smaller ones to establish a uniform two-and-one-quarter-inch outside diameter. Installation of the top rail would then be comparatively simple. The director of Recreation, Mike Haiday, was very cooperative and made the necessary financial arrangements and budgetary adjustments with the approval of City Manager Tom Hissom. Thus one of the apparent unattainable goals was reached, and the job of installing the top rail was easier than anticipated, thanks to Prunzie's triangular gadget used so successfully at the country club, to the cooperation of Mike Haiday, and the workmanship of Henry Lebejko.

While this was the last major function for the post straightener, the device, nonetheless, has since been used for minor work, and as recently as 1980. The top rail, of course, made it possible to attach desired shade curtains on the north fence, the stress on which has occasionally been too much for the posts from the junk yards. Sometimes the once discarded pipe has broken off completely just above the top of the concrete footings when bent back by the post straightener. But brain trust member and master handyman, Calvin Cobb, knows the answer to this problem—simply slide a smaller pipe, or sleeve, inside the broken post and pour in some cement from the top. Such a repair job is good for several decades, and the rejuvenated pipe, barring a holocaust, will not bend again.

18

The Final Two Courts at the Park—And with Lights

The next development at the Mohegan Park complex was a major one and far different from a pick-and-shovel operation or salvaging a broken junk yard fence post with poured concrete. It occurred in 1973 at the height of the tennis boom when interest in the game was at the apex of the popularity curve. For a time, at least, tennis was in the process of relinquishing its traditional role as the poor relation when the city council approved a departmental request of approximately $40,000 for additional tennis courts in the city of Norwich. The ordinance approved an allocation of $80,000 for recreational purposes from federal revenue-sharing funds, of which half was designated for six courts. The allocation provided for a single-court tennis facility in four critical areas throughout the city and also included provisions for two more clay courts at Mohegan Park. The playing surface for those in outlying districts was to be of bituminous construction. This was a wise decision, for maintenance of clay facilities in far-flung areas would be demanding to the point of absurdity. Hard tops would be the only plausible creations.

Clearly, the outburst of tennis interest and activity had impressed the councilmen, a couple of whom played the game fairly consistently. Council president, Konstant Morrel, was particularly instrumental in the action taken by the legislative body, which was favorably impressed with the success of the annual Southern New

England Tennis Championships. Many of the legislators were concerned with the decentralization of our tennis courts. Opportunities to play this great game would therefore be increased; concentration of all facilities in one area such as the park would preclude many from participation. The following semiurban places thus became the recipients of a tennis court: Taftville, Occum, Greenville, and the Yantic Lane area.

This advisory board member almost registered opposition to the single-isolated-court theory for a couple of reasons. First, higher construction costs would be involved in view of the necessity of setting up heavy equipment in four different areas. Installations of two courts would not only amount to much less cost per court, but also might make for a more sensible arrangement. As indicated earlier, a single facility inclines to discourage interest and participation in the game—particularly when contemplated as a recreational opportunity for a well-populated place. People come to play, find the court occupied, turn away, and many very probably never return. Moreover, traffic is limited to what one court can handle in any event and does not justify expenditure for supervision. Therefore, such a setup is apt to amount to a virtual private court for the few whose work and other schedules permit them to get to the place first.

However, it was thought better to get something than nothing in the respective areas, and suggested changes might lead to extended controversy and thus jeopardize the entire package. At the very least, more of the populace would see what a tennis court looked like, and perhaps a greater number might gain some knowledge of the game. Moreover, selected centrally located sites in Taftville and Greenville were adequate in size for but one court anyway. And the four single bituminous concrete courts with plexipave two-tone covering no doubt would satisfy a greater number of the key people who were interested in additional recreational facilities on a decentralized basis.

The results have been acceptable in some of the places, but one has to admit that insofar as tennis activity and opportunity is concerned a couple of the sites selected have been questionable. And the close proximity of basketball courts and various playground equipment often discourages those who wish to concentrate on their tennis games. There is no intention here of downgrading either outdoor basketball or playground equipment. On the contrary, in terms of usage and participation per square foot and per tax dollar, there are no better or more appropriate facilities. But when tennis courts are built too close to such installations they, along with the chain-link fences, are often utilized for various other recreational exercise—frequently while one is endeavoring to play the racket game.

None of these observations applies to the two additional clay courts at the park where there was room to the west to build parallel and in line with the existing four. (It has been necessary to renumber the six-court complex from left to right as one faces north from Mohegan Road. Thus, the newest ones have become "one" and "two," the first two built in 1950 "three" and "four," the others "five" and "six.") The expansion has made for a real enhancement and an excellent major tennis facility, and this despite some unfortunate developments that unfolded in the process of construction of "one" and "two."

Specifications for the first obvious, sensible approach to the building of municipal tennis courts in the Mohegan Park area with reasonably adequate and available funds were drawn up, as in the case of all similar governmental operations, by the engineering section of the Public Works Department. Understandably, and happily, at long last, the operation was not predicated upon gratuitous assistance from the volunteers of the brain trust nor did the "specs" contemplate use of materials that could be obtained free of charge, such as discarded pipe from the junk yards. Neither did they call for any pick-and-shovel exercise by a member of the Recreation Advisory Board nor for any associated advice.

The early phases of the construction work for the new courts "one" and "two" proceeded infallibly according to plan. Recreation director, Dick Fontaine, who had his maintenance personnel cut down trees in the area prior to the start of the operation, was very helpful here. The stumps were then removed by a heavy Caterpillar bulldozer, the place leveled with the same equipment, and bank gravel brought in for the base of the courts. The latter was graded with lighter machinery after which similar processed material was laid down on top preparatory for the final clay surface. This last layer of gravel was devoid of large stones, which, unlike the situation on courts "three," "four," "five," and "six," would otherwise eventually emerge through the clay surface.

Everything was working so smoothly, the huge dozer so effective, particularly in removing tree stumps, that any advice from a board member would have been ridiculous. It was far more appropriate simply to observe the tremendous superiority of twentieth-century equipment over the antiquated pick and shovel. The show was impressive and pointed up the relative folly and futility of the hand-tool operations used for the previous courts. The only suggestion by the board member was that there appeared to be too much overall pitch toward the catch basin outside the southwest gate behind court "three," but he was told that this was not the case.

None of this really bothered this advisory board member, for experience had taught that one is better off to adopt a low-key posture in respect to administrative personnel and those whom they engage. These individuals are apt to resent advice from lay people, which more often than not is construed as inappropriate interference. Moreover, members of the Recreation Advisory Board, as pointed out earlier, are not supposed to endeavor lateral negotiations at any stratum of the administrative pyramid. Their function is that of advising the city manager—at the pinnacle. Technically, it is only through the chief administrator that line or contracted personnel should be influenced or advised. And on top of this, everything was working so well in this case, like clockwork, that any interjected advice would be both unthinkable and superfluous. Again, one is better off to stay in the background, refrain from unsolicited suggestions, observe the result, and rectify anything unsatisfactory later—if, in fact, there is anything to rectify.

While such diplomatic behavior makes for harmonious relationships with all concerned, the strategy backfired this time, and this board member was in part responsible for a serious error in the make-up of the playing surface. He had remained too far in the background and was guilty of inattention. The smoothness and celerity that had characterized the procedure up to this point apparently had caused an unwarranted confidence and faith in the entire operation. The specifications supposedly had called for the integration of subsoil, or silt, with red clay from the brickyards as at the Home-Ec courts nearly four decades earlier. But the implausible had taken place. Yes, that fine sand so plentiful in area gravel banks was used instead of the less-accessible silt. No doubt there was a rationalization conceived by contractor and engineer that less red clay would be needed, that it was foolhardy to truck material forty miles from Middletown when adequate "clay" was close at hand. A considerable amount of the red clay from the brickyards was obtained, however, and was mixed in on the parking lot where the fine sand had been piled. A payloader was used for mixing purposes. The two architects are to be given credit for the introduction of some legitimate clay, for they easily could have made the gross error of using the fine sand exclusively. At any rate, this board member didn't "wise up" to what went on until it was too late, the components of this unique mixture having been brought in and integrated on the parking lot in his absence.

It surely appeared that this failure to engage in continual surveillance was unfortunate, for now there would be no other route except to cope with the fine sand. To remain in the background for the sake of harmony is one thing, but costly restraint solely in the name of accord is quite another. And the error seemed amplified when such reticence would cause the brain trust stalwarts additional work.

By far the greatest problem caused by the preponderance of the fine sand has been that of introducing and retaining adequate moisture in the surface. This is essential, for if it is not kept reasonably damp there is no firmness established and thus no tennis of consequence. The difficulty is compounded because of limitations in the water supply. When hosed from the existing source, pressure and volume are such that it is necessary to water the courts continuously in dry weather—once the job is completed you start all over again.

The answer to the problem, of course, is the introduction of calcium chloride, which acts as a binder, retains moisture, and makes for the requisite degree of solidification—eliminating the dust. Application of over one-half of a ton, or 1,000 pounds, per court per year has been about average. It doesn't matter a great deal what technique is employed so long as enough of the chloride permeates this unique surface. If each of the six clay courts required a comparable amount, one hesitates even to speculate where the resources, both funds and manpower, might come from. It would be extremely difficult to maintain the entire complex; the brain trust would be applying calcium chloride all summer—precluded from playing tennis.

There has been another difficulty with courts "one" and "two," in addition to the volume of chloride required. This has to do with the durability of the linseed-oil-and-traffic-paint lines, which do not adhere well to the sandy mixture. Linseed oil solidifies such a surface to the depth of its penetration, but that is it. There's no remaining bond. Thus the lines are not secure and peel off easily from the fine sand beneath. Therefore, it has been necessary to remove the material from all the areas where the lines go down, 480 linear feet per court, and trowel in legitimate clay. This operation, concluded in various stages over a few years, has solved this problem, and the lines now remain firm when applied to the new material.

Some additional minor tasks are involved in the maintenance of the two courts. Occasionally, ruts and gulleys will appear after heavy rains, but these are readily filled with new clay. It's a procedure that, if continued extensively enough, will result in a comparatively new and satisfactory surface for courts "one" and "two." Another problem has arisen, which relates to the high degree of pitch from west to east. Many of the lines on court "two" become obliterated and buried from surface material that is washed down from court "one" during rainstorms. There's just enough clay in the mixture to cause it to stick like glue to the inundated lines of the second court. Sweeping the stuff off with rugged brooms, uncovering the lines so they become visible once again, is frequently a task of the first magnitude. Would that contractor and engineer were available to assist in this operation.

So much has been written about the negative aspects of the new tennis facilities that the reader will be pleased to learn that there's an important positive side. The courts have advantageous characteristics that, to some degree, exonerate both contractor and engineer. Tennis players, tournament committees, and the brain trust are all appreciative beneficiaries of certain special properties of the two courts, for there are times when they are a real plus, when we are thankful they were built on an inclined plane. It is because court "one" has turned out to be one of the fastest-drying courts in existence. The pitch from west to east is such that all rainwater runs off the surface immediately, creating puddles on the north and south ends of court "two". What water remains on the top of "one" is absorbed almost instantaneously. (It is usually in dire need of moisture anyway.) Therefore, thanks to the combination of its unique composition and excessive pitch, we have one clay facility that can be used very soon after rains, light or heavy. (Court "two" is not far behind, but here it's necessary to sweep out the puddles.) And many have been the occasions when the fast-drying "one" was a real asset. Frequently, as any seasoned tournament chairman knows, the competition is held up, postponed, almost ruined because of rain. Court "one," sometimes playable as much as a full day ahead of the rest, has aided this situation—particularly if a tournament is stalled about the time of the semifinals, or in fact even the finals, when occasionally a cloudburst will arrive upon the scene when the match is halfway along. The game is simply transferred to "one" when the rain stops.

The Tournament Committee will not forget the recent championships in 1981, which were plagued by almost continual precipitation and intermittent downpours. Anyone who might have seen the tennis courts the night before the final day of the tournament after a severe cloudburst that occurred would have stated flatly that match play would be postponed for at least a fortnight. Yet in the morning of that very next day we were rolling courts "one" and "two" preparatory for the day's play. They would be ready even before any hard-surface courts, which would be loaded with puddles. Committee member Bill Stevens, who has done a great job scheduling the matches the last several years, as did Paul Morosky before him, was positively flabbergasted when told he could put the show on the road. John Tauro, another dedicated member of the committee, forthwith posted the draw sheets, and Jeannie Shannon was surprised to learn that she would have the data to complete the voluminous paperwork associated with a sanctioned tournament on schedule so she could get to the beach on time for a planned vacation.

Perhaps, after all, both the contractor and engineer had in mind all along construction of the fastest-drying courts in the country. If so, they succeeded famously. But the combination of excessive pitch from west to east and the unique surface of fine sand, which has made for playability almost immediately after rains, does not really offset the difficulties of maintenance already covered. Neither does it detract from the mistakes and omissions of which this board member is guilty, for there was no real excuse for not being on top of the fine sand fiasco before it was too late.

There was probably another similar error in connection with the fence, which turned out to be ten rather than twelve feet in height. The construction job appeared to be fairly simple. After removal of the fence immediately to the west of court "three," the proposition was simply that of building extensions to the existing structure, now embellished with a top rail, on the north and south ends, and enclosing once again to the west. Funds would be available for new two-inch black iron pipe for posts in lieu of those from the junk yard this time. Two standard twenty-one-foot lengths of new pipe when cut and coupled are adequate for three posts of fourteen feet each, allowing for a more than acceptable two-foot insertion into the concrete footings. After the posts are leveled at proper height and lined up satisfactorily, loop caps slip readily over the top of the uprights after the cement sets. Inch-and-a-quarter black iron pipe for the top rail slips easily through the loops. Any type of fencing, expensive or otherwise, may then be attached to this framework, which should be painted green—making for a good-looking job. This is precisely what we wound up with, utilizing discarded pipe from junk yards and Henry Lebejko's workmanship. However, in this instance, one-and-one-quarter-inch galvanized pipe, which bends fairly readily, was used instead for the ten-foot uprights.

Since few take much notice of fences surrounding tennis courts, particularly at Mohegan Park where the green posts and top rail blend into the background of trees and foliage, one might say that the case for uniformity of height is overstated. It is probably true that the aesthetic aspect here can be overemphasized, and it is possible to be too much of a perfectionist. After all, it's the courts themselves and playability of the surface that count. So long as a fence fulfills the major function of keeping tennis balls within the premises, it is satisfactory. Assuming all this to be true, however, there are other limitations in this new ten-foot fence versus the old, which have to do with relative structural strength. The one-and-one-quarter-inch galvanized uprights are not strong enough, and they bend easily from heavy winds when shade curtains are attached. Already it has been necessary to turn to Prunzie's post-straightening device on more than one occasion. Happily, this gadget is still available, for otherwise we would be required to forego curtains on the north end of courts "one" and "two." There would be no question in such case that this result would not only be unaesthetic but also undesirable. Thus the only solution, not as straightforward as other problems, is to remove the comparatively new fence and build another one. It is something that this board member would like to see come to pass one day.

However, the reticent advisory board member did not stand by quietly throughout the entire project, for there was one important part of the undertaking where his impact was far greater than anything verbal or advisory. There occurred a mobilization on a Sunday morning that spring in 1974 of a few stalwarts of the brain trust who rolled up their sleeves and tackled one phase of the job directly. By sundown the task was completed, the end of a tough Sabbath work day, as Dick Korenkiewicz and Tom Winters will testify. When the fence contractor arrived Monday morning together with tools and equipment ready to do the work he was dumbfounded as he observed the fait accompli.

This unsanctioned maneuver involved the moving of all eight of the net posts on courts "three," "four," "five," and "six" a few feet in the easterly direction. At a meeting of the Zoning Board of Appeals, and after listening to the resident immediately to the west on Mohegan Road object to the proximity of proposed courts "one" and "two" to his home, this board member had suggested the relocation of the four courts slightly to the east, as much as space would permit. This idea was acceptable to all concerned even though the distance between the new court "one" and the property line would not be increased very much. The neighbor, who made it clear that he had nothing against tennis or added facilities in the area, had suggested expansion of the complex in the opposite direction, but this would necessitate new construction on an elevated level as well as eliminating a substantial portion of the much-needed parking area.

The relocation of the net posts had been allocated to the fence contractor who was at his wits' end as to how to accomplish the job without bringing heavy equipment onto the playing surface. The board member tried to convince the contractor that the operation could be done with hand tools but to no avail. In retrospect, we were fortunate that the contractor's impasse occurred on a Friday afternoon, for it meant that Saturday could be devoted to speculation and experimentation while leaving all day Sunday for the formidable task. We were also lucky that good weather prevailed throughout the weekend.

There was no easy way to separate the net posts from the concrete footings, and therefore it was best to dig out the current base, pull out the entire footing somehow, and lower it all into the new freshly dug hole. Saturday's successful trial with a selected post turned out to be an easier assignment than anticipated. We knew that it wouldn't be too difficult to dig around the footing, but we were uncertain about our ability to pull it out onto the court surface. However, by laying down a six-foot crowbar and attaching the center to the net post, it was found that two rugged stalwarts could readily lift up the whole unit with one laborer on each end of the bar. In fact, the most difficult part of the operation was that of setting up the post properly in its new residence. Both height and alignment of net posts are critical in tennis. The top of the pulley at the upper extremity of the post has to be exactly forty-two inches above the surface, and obviously each upright must stand perpendicular to and line up satisfactorily with all the others. It is also essential to tamp the replaced footing securely so that it will remain at a ninety-degree angle with the level of the courts when the net cable is drawn taut.

Apprehension with respect to these important details plus downright panic over the prospect of a payloader chewing up the clay surface caused three ambitious brain trusters to endeavor the relocation of the seven other posts the next day on the Sabbath. It was a tough but rewarding day's work, completed at dusk. And the transplanted posts have remained firm, secure, and perpendicular to this day at the conclusion of the 1984 season. An explanatory letter to the finance office of the city written by this advisory board member was sufficient to subtract an appropriate amount from the fence contractor's stipend. Thus ended another extralegal exercise. None of the unexpended funds wound up in the pockets of the brain trusters.

With the completion of the ten-foot fence around the new courts "one" and "two," together with required conditioning work on their sandy surfaces, the city of Norwich became the recipient of a six-court clay tennis complex. This now major facility not only stimulated interest in the game and allowed for a great deal more play, but also simplified the running of tournaments. No longer did we need the courts at the country club for the Southern New England Tennis Championships. But the complex had not yet reached its present stage, for there was one more important embellishment to come, namely, the installation of lights. The new development was initiated and passed by the city council with no suggestion, influence, pressure, or extralegal activity on the part of the Recreation Advisory Board or any of its members. This enhancement came at an opportune time in 1975 and 1976—opportune because the idea of lights never would have been favorably received and subsequently passed unless tennis interest was at a high level on the curve and also because it all took place over a two-year span (half the courts were lighted in 1975, the remaining three in 1976), just before both government and the general public became aroused with respect to the curtailment and conservation of energy.

The president pro tempore of the city council, Jim Calkins, was the driving force behind the project, and by his own admission. In fact, one day at the courts, well after installation of the lights, the president pro tempore, who had a high interest in tennis and who played a good game, remarked in jest to this board member that while "they may be the Armstrong courts, they're the Calkins lights." A more accurate observation in respect to the lights could not be made.

As previously indicated, this board member adopted a hands-off policy, refraining from exercising any pressure or influence in favor or otherwise. While outwardly responding to interrogations and inquiries with positive enthusiasm, deep down there were mixed feelings about the undertaking. Though pleased that the tennis project was held in such high regard as to warrant a major expenditure, one nonetheless had some misgivings and even a slight feeling of guilt. In one sense it seemed incongruous to illuminate the handmade area with a preponderance of stones and fine sand in the playing surface—a twentieth-century implementation exposing nineteenth-century makeshift workmanship. Yet in another sense the idea of lights not only sounded good but also well worth the expenditure; they would be particularly advantageous in the autumn months when evening daylight hours are fewer.

Anyone who has observed the fine Norwich Free Academy girls tennis program in the fall, particularly an interscholastic match in late October, would acquiesce in favor of the expenditure. This excellent program, capably run by Sarah Jane Shearer, physical education supervisor, encompasses both varsity and junior varsity competition, and lights are indispensable for this extensive activity. Without them, there simply would not be enough time before dark to run the important junior varsity matches. First-team competition doesn't get under way until after school is out—about 3:00 P.M.

The lights, which, as in the case of courts "one" and "two," were funded by council allocation of federal revenue sharing, also have proved very helpful in connection with the running of tournaments, both local and sectional. While it is infrequent that any matches are actually scheduled to start under the lights, very often matches are completed under them. The Tournament Committee is thus relieved of that perennial bugbear, namely, confrontations that are halted because of darkness. To say that the absence of unfinished matches, which otherwise would have to be completed the following morning, fouling up that day's schedule, facilitates the running of tournaments is a gross understatement.

Thus the lights, which illuminate the courts from posts spaced along the outside of the north and south fences, have been extremely helpful quite apart from the extension of playing time for the populace in general. And there are many of our citizens, previously unable to play much tennis owing to work day commitments, who are now able to spend more time on the courts. Some play under the lights exclusively.

It is interesting that the cost of each one of the good-looking, tapererd and cylindrical, thirty-foot iron light posts was appreciably in excess of the total appropriation of $500 in 1953 for courts "five" and "six" combined. (There are fourteen posts in all, seven on each of the north and south sides.) But such are the implausibilities that only history can explain away. The posts have been painted green and are hardly noticeable in daylight hours.

However, the lights are somewhat inadequate in respect to illumination capability, and this is why tournament matches are seldom scheduled after dark. As in many such installations, the lighting is not sufficient for good visibility in the difficult twilight hours. Illumination improves later on when the sun is completely down. Even then the older veteran players whose vision is not what it was in youth seldom play under lights. Perhaps in time better lenses will be available, requiring the same amount of, or even less, electrical energy.

19

The Fruition of Efforts of the Recreation Department and the Brain Trust

None of the unfortunate developments at the six-court tennis complex has been irreconcilably tragic, however. And even though no improvement in the lights will be forthcoming in the forseeable future, they are fairly adequate and represent a beneficial addition. And the task of getting rid of the fine sand on courts "one" and "two" is not infinite, thanks to the combination of wind and rain, routine brushing, shovel and hoe—together with timely replacement of the weak areas with real clay. Then, too, the annual spring stone-removal workout on courts "three," "four," "five," and "six" is becoming somewhat simplified, partly because of gradual improvement in technique in the provocative endeavor, and also because so many stones have been thrown out over the years, their previous abode filled with clay, that the remaining amalgamated gravel-and-clay playing area has become diminished. This stone-slinging preseason exercise amounts to a perpetual rejuvenation of the surface of the courts and has the important result of postponing the day when a complete resurfacing project becomes necessary. The clay from Asylum Avenue and Sterling Mott's farm cannot last indefinitely. It continually dwindles from winds and cloudbursts, except for the stones, which neither disintegrate nor blow away. Probably no more than 30 or 40 percent of the original amount delivered back in the early 1950s remains. Periodic introduction of new clay is thus imperative. And if this is done consistently and extensively, an overall resurfacing project will not be on the agenda for some time.

All of this proves not only that an acceptable facility can emerge from any given beginning, even fine sand, but also that any field or court, baseball diamond or playground, demands almost constant attention. There's always a chore to be done, and there is usually something that can be done to improve a facility regardless of its state or condition. While these observations are particularly applicable to clay tennis courts, the same can be said in respect to any complex—even bituminous surfaces. In addition, almost anyone, if so disposed, can perform maintenance functions on a clay court. The same may not be said of a hardtop, however. As observed previously, the tendency is to build the hard courts rather than clay because of the continual maintenance requirements, as opposed to the infrequent rehabilitations bituminous or concrete surfaces demand. This, among other things, if an individual is a bona-fide enthusiast, is one of the advantages of clay—particularly for a private facility. The owner always has something to do besides playing tennis.

A few clay courts are appropriate for municipalities, too, if for no other reason than to provide better conditions for the middle-aged and older participants. Hard courts are tough on the feet and legs, they draw heat, and are too hot at midday in summer months. Moreover, the upkeep of clay courts is good healthy work for municipal maintenance personnel. Park employees are ever mowing grass, pruning rose gardens, and what have you. Why not condition clay courts? Enough bituminous material is being applied anyway—for roads and highways, parking areas, etc. The earth would be an uninteresting planet if completely blacktopped. And satisfactorily maintained clay courts are an asset to any city.

However, if such facilities require more than a reasonable amount of maintenance they are undesirable for a municipality or other institution. Therefore, the importance of optimum initial construction on this score cannot be overemphasized. The folly of the introduction of fine sand in the surface of courts "one" and "two" may be highlighted here just once again. The problems involved in maintaining courts "three" and "four" are not as great, but they are becoming more severe, particularly on court "four," where the gravel-and-clay mixture is becoming predominantly gravel in too many places. A major introduction of clay is increasingly imperative. This hopefully will be on the agenda soon and shouldn't take maintenance personnel very long, with perhaps an assist from some available volunteers. A complete resurfacing project is not necessary; simple replacement of the exposed gravel with clay, while keeping the same grade and level, is all that is required.

The situation on courts "five" and "six" is fortunately totally different. These are among the best municipal clay courts to be found anywhere, and they handle more traffic than the others, almost twice as much. There are many occasions when players arrive to play tennis when all the courts are vacant, as for example, very early in the morning—like 6:00 A.M., or on very hot days at midday. Obviously, these racket wielders have their choice of courts, and they invariably select either "five" or "six." Moreover, all tournament finals are held on one or the other, and not just because of better spectator potential from bleachers on the bank next to the parking area. In the late 1970s "Chip" Spiller from Florida International College in Miami, and a ranking player in that state, entered the Southern New England Tennis Championships and played his first match on number "five." After conclusion of the game "Chip" stated that it was one of the best clay courts he had ever played on. He was told that his entry would be accepted for any subsequent tournament in which he would like to participate here. No one asked "Chip" whether he would be equally complimentary had he lost the match.

It is not meant to imply that the other four courts are poor, for when properly maintained they play about as well as "five" and "six." But these two represent the heart of the complex and it's nice that they are first class. The courts, unlike the rest, require little or no maintenance, and virtually no calcium chloride needs to be introduced into the playing surface. This has been a fortunate development; if such were not the case, if every court required the same treatment as number "one," for example, maintenance of the entire establishment would hardly be worth the effort. Courts "five" and "six" not only are the best of the six at Mohegan Park, but also are by far the least expensive. It will be recalled that the $500 appropriation in 1953 for the facilities was adequate only for the fences at the north and south ends, consummation of which requiring procurement of the posts from junk yards. The story is that the brain trust people who built the two courts simply lucked out in this instance, and unwittingly. Because of the gradual elevation of the terrain to the east of the first two courts built in 1950, no gravel was brought in for the base of "five" and "six." Removal of the topsoil had brought the level of this section of the earth down to that of the gravel base of "three" and "four." The intelligentsia had decided to try to come up with a satisfactory playing area by treating the place as it was, after being stripped and leveled by the city grader. Later, a four- or five-inch layer of clay from Sterling Mott's farm was applied, it will be remembered. All of which amounted to the construction of two courts in the gradual incline of a natural bank. Thus the courts are fortunately the beneficiary of the water table from surrounding land and their surface never dries to the point that it becomes dusty. Consequently, calcium chloride is seldom needed. Moreover, the underground below the clay is apparently of sufficient make-up and porosity as to afford adequate drainage after rains; the degree of moisture is just about right and remains fairly constant. Thus the surface stays firm and playable, with no appreciable maintenance work being required. Would that upkeep on all the courts was equally minimal.

No two of the six municipal courts are exactly alike from the maintenance standpoint, however. There are differences even between "five" and "six." Some of the gravel brought in by Selectman Dorsey extends under the west side of court "five," for example. There is no uniform or common base. Two feet of bank gravel resides under court "three" (necessary to fill up the old water hole), there's less under number "four," and none under most of "five" and all of "six." Thus the amount of calcium chloride to be applied varies from court to court, and some require more repair work than others, and need to be rolled more often.

Any capable maintenance employee learns this routine in short order. But the difficulty has been that once an individual becomes familiar with the work and skilled in its performance, we invariably lose him. He has found a better-paying job elsewhere. Moreover, when the CETA program (Comprehensive Employment Training Act) was in vogue, the tenure of the workers was limited by law. The incessant turnover understandably has made for a perennial problem, that of the annual effort involved in training new personnel. This has not been a simple, straightforward, uncomplicated task, for it is fair to say that there are some who have proved to be untrainable. But there are always, as in any group, significant others, like staff members Ray Szalkowski and Ray Daley for whom one go-around or demonstration is good for all time. The same applies to an exceptional group of young men, all students happy to obtain summer employment working on the tennis courts. Vin Cerillo, Dave Kozak, Rich Moran, Eric Dupont, and Mike Fusaro have worked for the department in this capacity at various times during the last fifteen years, and each has acquired the basic court maintenance technique quickly and has done fine work. One of these young people has been hired every summer and each has been retained until graduation from college or until permanently employed elsewhere. The job entails work on evenings and weekends when the courts require both surveillance and consistent upkeep.

However, many are those who are assigned to spring conditioning work whose capabilities lie somewhere between the proficient and the untrainable. These workers need incessant supervision and, though their hearts are in the right place, they are forever applying linseed oil on the wrong side of the guidelines and stumbling over the spikes before they are driven down, necessitating both repair and remeasurement. But here again there are noteworthy exceptions. Some employees, Larry Sirpenski and Raoul Santana, for instance, have become enthusiastic to a remarkable degree; they have actually returned to the courts on weekends to lend a hand gratuitously. Would that there were more job opportunities in this technological age that could incorporate such a nonperfunctory aspect. One can readily appreciate the motivation of some of the tennis players like Attorney Stan Yorsz and Dr. Tom Winters, who have pitched in consistently over the years—during vacations and holidays and after classes while in high school. But for one on the payroll to come back to help on his day off is a rarity of the first magnitude. Yet it's impossible to retain young men like Larry and Raoul, for they cannot be expected to work indefinitely for minimum wage.

Inevitable changes in personnel also have occurred in municipal administration—from the city manager on down. One who has been a member of the Recreation Advisory Board since the introduction of the council-manager form of government early in 1952 has obviously dealt with each of the managers in the city's history. But some have not been in office long enough to become acquainted with the board—to say nothing of grappling with the important problems and considerations in the Recreation Department. Fortunately, the current city manager, Charles Whitty, has not only been around long enough to be knowledgeable about departmental operations, but he has served (and still does) as a volunteer in recreational activities. Charlie currently is manager of a senior Little League baseball team—as well as being manager of the city. In general, however, and from a long-range viewpoint, the turnover in chief administrators has not been helpful in the field of recreation, particularly in respect to the construction of municipal clay tennis courts.

There have also been turnovers in directors of Recreation, but the changes in this position have been fewer than that of city manager. Each one of the five directors in Norwich who had held the top administrative job in the department have been dedicated to their work and the field of recreation. All have had to handle the difficult task of relating to volunteers and dovetailing activities accordingly. They all have realized that recreation is so broad a field that no one can be thoroughly knowledgeable in all areas. Norwich is fortunate that the current director, Richard Fontaine, is well qualified on this score. He is mature enough and experienced in the field of recreation, to which he has devoted much of his life, to have acquired a good overall perspective. Dick not only has a healthy attitude, but he comes through when the "chips are down," providing both manpower, materials, and equipment when they are needed. Moreover, his spirit of cooperation has become transmitted throughout the entire permanent staff, which is the best in the history of the department. Foreman Neil Bresnan, maintenance men Bill Barry and Peter Doroschevich, and secretary Cathy Pineault are all dedicated and capable. There is no intention here of casting reflection on previous workmen or inferring limitations, for virtually all have been devoted and committed employees. Joe Boucher, as noted earlier, worked seven days a week, for example, and once stayed up until 4:00 A.M. building an umpire stand for the tournament finals the ensuing day. There's something inherent in recreational endeavor that frequently causes one to work beyond the call of duty.

Rather it is the story of a department that has finally become of age, operating today under a more sensible and realistic budget, and with its own maintenance department. Dependence upon Public Works for upkeep of the many areas and fields involved has been discarded long since. When this board member was originally appointed in 1952, the annual budget was in the neighborhood of $15,000; the fiscal 1982-1983 appropriation for Recreation in the city of Norwich is $262,088. The department, here as elsewhere, enjoys at long last genuine status as a legitimate governmental function, and its financial resources are becoming closer to what the programs and activities require.

But the resources, both monetary and available manpower, are not as yet sufficient to maintain the gravel, sand, and clay tennis courts as well as every other recreational area. There is still an important function and need for whatever volunteer help that is available. While the demand for this assistance is now less critical, the proposition of satisfactory maintenance of the courts is not a reasonable or justifiable assignment for the staff. It would be quite possible to assign the conditioning and upkeep of the courts to the three permanent employees on a full-time basis at certain times during the year, particularly in the spring—leaving them no time to attend the various fields and playgrounds. The same could be said in respect to other facilities—for example, the excellent new soccer field, now Fontaine Field. There is no end to the general care required for any such area if one is a perfectionist. Dickenman Field, the major baseball diamond, is another case in point.

What foreman Bresnan has to do, therefore, is assign the men practically and expediently so that all the fields and grounds will be maintained in some kind of reasonable condition. He must refrain from being too much of a perfectionist. His resources—men, materials, and equipment—necessarily require a somewhat thin application across a considerable portion of the topography of the municipality. Perennial problems are in evidence at virtually every baseball and softball field (three baseball and four softball fields come under the jurisdiction of the department), as well as at any one of the fifteen playgrounds—to say nothing of the fourteen outdoor hardtop basketball courts. These places take an incessant and severe pounding from sheer use alone, and in this day and age they are also subject to frequent acts of vandalism, which only compound the gigantic task of maintenance. Small wonder there are ample opportunities for ambitious, civic-minded volunteers in recreation, including the resourceful brain trust of the tennis courts.

It is easy to see, therefore, that important emphasis is to be placed upon the relationships between volunteers and administrative personnel. The goal is, or should be, the achievement of optimum coordination, which frequently is more difficult to attain than one might think. This objective is apt to be somewhat more elusive if one is both a volunteer and a policy-maker—such as this member of the Recreation Advisory Board. The fact that municipal clay courts are involved, where a substantial portion of the upkeep is done gratuitously, makes this relationship a matter of consequence, for a policy-maker is probably doubly interested in getting things done. In this effort he must be careful not to step on the toes of administrators or foremen and avoid the invasion and usurpation of their jurisdiction and authority. This is precisely where both Dick Fontaine and Neil Bresnan rate high in the estimation of this board member. Their employees are handled adroitly in this sometimes delicate situation so that they work harmoniously with the pseudo-boss.

There are two routes that a policy-maker interested in accomplishment in the recreation field may take: one verbal, one manual. The former calls for meetings, discussions, and perhaps ultimate resolutions; the latter for direct confrontation, for overt assault on the project itself—occasionally with pick and shovel as in the moving of the eight net posts at Recreation Field. Over the years this has been the avenue elected, and it has proven effective from the standpoint both of facilitating relationships and of getting things done. Almost no one discounts straightforward hard work and associated sweat—though there are many who very likely believe this procedure to be foolhardy, that there must be a better and easier way. But ample evidence can be found that substantiates and justifies this approach insofar as the longevity of clay tennis courts is concerned, public or otherwise. And tennis courts, though somewhat unique in this respect, are not the only recreational facilities where such direct effort prevails, for there are very many individuals who have devoted much of their lives to the enhancement and enrichment of other programs and activities, gratuitously, frequently involving actual physical work on the fields as at the tennis courts. The efforts of these unsung heroes, cohorts in recreation, are profoundly appreciated here.

Direct involvement on the part of citizens varies, of course, with the size of the community and the degree to which recreation departments have become established. One would be foolishly adventurous to attempt the construction and maintenance of clay tennis courts in a large metropolitan area by hand. While cities, towns, and other governmental units differ from one another, no two being exactly alike, some general observations can be made that relate to their size, nevertheless. In a small town, councilmen or selectmen may want actually to drive a fire truck or operate other equipment prior to its purchase, while such a consideration would not enter the mind of a similar governmental official in a big city. Thus the functions of policy-makers and the degree of their involvement in administrative matters differs from place to place, understandable in part in view of respective populations. The dividing line between policy formation together with those responsible for its formulation, on the one hand, and the carrying out of that planning by departmental personnel varies widely. In a city the size of Norwich, with its singular history, attitudes, and propensities, it can be stated that the line of demarcation between the functions of policy-makers and those of administrators, particularly in the Department of Recreation, is not sharply defined. Here the official duties of dispensation of advice at board meetings and active engagement in projects with tools and equipment are not incompatible.

The history of the emergence of the handmade municipal tennis courts in Mohegan Park is not confined to the special adaptations of the council-manager form of government, for there are untold other determining factors. It is the sum total of the accidents of construction and surface composition together with many other influences, the ingredients and antecedents if you will, that explain away this unique result—just as in the case of the history of anything else. Hopefully, the foregoing story has suggested some of the important determining forces here. Given the long-time status of the game as a poor relation, both in athletic circles and in municipal recreation, and given the associated lack of available resources, together with other significant factors, it probably can be concluded that there could be no other general way the existence of the complex could have come to pass, four courts as early as 1954.

It is true, no doubt, that some unfortunate decisions were made as well as errors and omissions in judgment and advice. There could and should have been an improvement in surveillance of courts "one" and "two." This board member could have done a lot of other things in connection with earlier situations. He could have initiated special meetings, spent more time in sedentary repose around the conference table, enticing more people into the project. Or one could have adopted a totally different approach, for example, the launching of drives to obtain money from interested citizens. Or he could have concentrated on the accumulation of personal funds and made a substantial gift. If such a donation were adequate in size to construct the entire facility, in the estimation of many it might have been more impressive than the monetary value of the hours and years of hard work involved. And as philosophers, legitimate and curbstone, have pointed out, such a gift endowment has a more ethical connotation as well as being held in higher regard.

But then the tennis courts would have had a different history and their construction less fun for many individuals. The opportunity to work with municipal employees and CETA workers would not have taken place, and we would not have been recipients of one of the fastest-drying courts in the world. Moreover, the esprit de corps engendered among working cohorts, the unforgettable association with the brain trust, could not have transpired, nor would have the educational and philosophical weekly sessions over fifteen-cent libation. Those who comprised this unofficial group had considerable influence on the project, particularly the original membership in the early 1950s—that of Ted Montgomery being significant. Ted's patience and dedication at the West Side Tennis Court on Forest Street had a positive and profound effect on the boys. His unflagging preoccupation with that court clearly demonstrated that an acceptable facility eventually will become manifest regardless of the starting point and subsequent difficulties encountered. Then there was the early interest and participation of the chairman of the Recreation Commission in 1950, Jim Pedace, who gave the undertaking its initial impetus. His everlasting devotion to the improvement of the city and recreational opportunities in particular set the tone of the entire operation. Though not one of the group referred to here as the "brain trust" and never in attendance at the Sunday afternoon philosophical sessions, Jim's role in the early years was very important, nonetheless. And later, when the rejuvenation of the Home-Ec courts took place, the boys not only gained the acquaintance of Judge Allyn Brown but also enjoyed his approval of their efforts. Working next to the prestigious judge, always busy in his backyard adjacent to the courts, and appreciating his interest and encouragement was an experience the volunteers looked forward to and which gave them a genuine assurance, which carried over to the park as well.

While many have been those who have influenced the course and consummation of the project, no doubt some of consequence who regrettably have not been mentioned in this story, there is one category worthy of note before it's too late. It has been impossible to identify the individual members, for the group is unknown and apparently operates effectively in complete oblivion. Reference is made to those elusive workmen called "they." Throughout thirty-one years on the advisory board, this member has listened to accolades and tributes paid to "they" hundreds of times, and convincingly to the point where he almost believed in the existence of such a maintenance corps. One spring, after finishing the line-painting job on court "one" and while actually engaged in the same procedure on court "two," an onlooker, the NFA tennis coach, no less, remarked that "they" did a good job on the first court. There is a rather vague but real assumption by many that there exists an efficient, knowledgeable staff behind the scene somewhere, which is dedicated to timely accomplishment. This is particularly true of governmental operations. But though street and highway crews that frequently do much of their work at night are not directly observed and are understandably referred to as "they," painted lines on municipal tennis courts are not laid down in the dark.

Though enough space has been allocated previously to this line-painting procedure, perhaps too much, it is thought appropriate to make one or two additional points. The linseed-oil-and-traffic-paint method, if done properly, not only has resulted in good-looking courts but also has stimulated the workers, both volunteers and many municipal employees. There is nothing more encouraging for workmen than a clean-cut, attractive result. And when they begin to take pride in their efforts and labor the battle is won.

It would be erroneous to say that the finished product, after the courts are conditioned and lined, does not act as a stimulant for this advisory board member also. The sense of accomplishment assists no end when it comes time for the repainting or "touching up" process. When the courts are maintained in first-class shape, which of course requires consistent attention to the lines, it makes all the effort involved worthwhile. It could be that the academic background in mathematics and Euclidean geometry at the Norwich Free Academy and Brown University has had something to do with the special cognizance and importance ascribed to a good-looking clay tennis court with straight lines exactly perpendicular to one another. No higher mathematics is involved in establishing accurate intersections, and if one follows available instructions, a knowledge of the Pythagorean theorem is not necessary, for any capable schoolboy can measure out a tennis court. But if one has some appreciation of the right triangle and the relationship of the hypotenuse to its other two sides he is less apt to do a botch job.

Then there was the early twentieth-century work on the farm and in the construction of buildings of various kinds during the Great Depression where by today's standards both tools and equipment were antiquated. The major implements were the pick and shovel, hammer, and hand saw. For the most part, these were the only tools available to the pre-Wimbledon progenitor in those days. One inclines to tackle his undertakings utilizing methods and procedures with which he is familiar—hence the preponderance of the use of the pick and shovel in the construction of the municipal tennis courts.

Once the job was initiated and the bank gravel integrated with the clay it became predicated upon the continued employment of outmoded techniques. When the gravel-and-clay combination became the playing surface there was no recourse, short of starting from scratch again, but to throw out the protruding stones each spring by hand. However, the result is satisfactory and the surface tough and durable, and justifies the effort and labor involved. It's uninteresting work, but happily this general situation is improving.

Way back, a member of the brain trust organization theorized that we appreciate the courts all the more because of the tedious work required each spring. There is a great deal of truth in this observation, and more can be added. In this day and age, few opportunities exist that offer similar experience, which is probably regrettable. Modern technology is such and equipment so advanced and sophisticated as to rule out the possibility. One supposes this to be inevitable, that hand-tool operations and work assignments like throwing out stones would not satisfy the multitudinous requirements imposed by a complex society and economy. While this is also true, and though it is both impossible and probably inappropriate to turn the clock back, clay tennis courts, those at Mohegan Park in particular, are a noteworthy exception. The people themselves haven't changed basically. Everyone still thrives upon gaining a sense of accomplishment from expenditure of effort and energy, whatever the limitations in a highly complicated world.

Accordingly, the municipal clay tennis courts have offered a comparatively rare opportunity. And it is one of the exceptional aspects about involvement in the field of recreation—the more true in a city of the size and history of Norwich, Connecticut. Few are the situational and environmental settings where one who might wish to make some kind of a contribution along this line has the chance of so doing. Most people would not know where to begin. Everyone is quite aware of the growing need for more meaningful human experience, and the writer is not so naive as to suggest that preoccupation with clay tennis courts can provide much of an increment here. But even though the municipal complex at Mohegan Park comprises only 36,000 square feet of the surface of the earth, its perpetuation and maintenance represents a plus for humankind, however infinitesimal. Moreover, the advantages of association with such a project are both uncomplex and visible, uncomplex because one can be sure of his direction, and visible because the result comes clearly into view. And so such work and involvement is really an easy and certain way to make a contribution, and the philosophers of the brain trust together with the Recreation Department steadfastly have operated on this simple premise—with apologies for the looks of the tennis courts early each spring.

Epilogue

Since the text of this book was completed, the 26th annual Southern New England Tennis Tournament has been concluded with new champions crowned and there have been changes in some of the tennis areas which took place very recently in the summer of 1984.

First, at the Norwich Inn, tennis is once again on the agenda, two excellent well lighted Har Tru courts having been built. This facility, constructed by Tim Reid of Windsor, Connecticut was not built on the site of the original courts since the Inn no longer owns the golf course, but is located much closer to the Inn itself, near the parking area.

Also the Home-Ec courts are no longer owned by the Norwich Free Academy. In fact, owing to a decreasing enrollment there has been available space on the campus proper for the Home-Ec program since 1978. At that time the Home-Ec building was leased to the Learning Lab, a successful accelerated grammar school. The projected outlook in respect to enrollment continues to be such that NFA will not need the Home-Ec complex in the forseeable future. Thus, the Academy has recently sold the building, including the tennis courts, to the Learning Lab.

Joe Booquin, playing the best tennis of his life, won the 1984 Southern New England tennis title for the first time. He prevailed in a field that was dominated by precocious youth, such as 16-year-old Gordie Ernst of Cranston, R.I. The 34-year-old veteran showed too much experience and patience for the hard hitting youngsters. Joe won the semi finals over formidable Paul Arciero 6-1, 6-0, and in the finals defeated Kurt Lichtman, a Big Ten intercollegiate player from the University of Michigan, 6-4, 6-0. Heather Eldredge returned to Norwich and successfully recaptured the Women's singles title defeating up-and-coming Ann Corcoran of Palmer, Mass. in the finals 6-4, 4-6, 6-2. Miss Eldredge is now a sophomore at the University of Texas where last year, as a freshman, she played #3 on the varsity team.

There was a surprising, yet very gratifying development in the men's doubles competition in which Norwich's unseeded team of Dave Coletti and Mislav Coric won three successive three-set matches in the quarterfinals, semifinals and finals to emerge as champions. This result was most exciting for it was the first time local players had won any major title in the men's division. Coletti is a sophomore at Boston University and Coric, a 1984 Norwich Free Academy graduate, will be a freshman at Duke University in January of 1985.